SILENT ASSASSINS SOCIETY

CYBER HUNTER ORIGINS BOOK 4

D. B. GOODIN

For more information about the Cyber Hunter Origins series visit:

www.cyberhunterorigins.com

www.dbgoodinbooks.com

www.davidgoodinauthor.com

ISBN: 9798215495766 (Paperback)

CHAPTER 1

ATLANTIC CITY, May 30, 1929

Soon it would be all over for her, as it was for so many others. Ah, how he loved the forgotten runaways. He smiled at the woman next to him as he approached the boardwalk city. She was a plain woman he'd picked up in some forgotten town in Kansas. Or was it New Hampshire? He couldn't remember. Midas Mink drove his new Dodge Senior Six along the Atlantic Coast Highway. He was in a fantastic mood. Everyone said it couldn't be done, but he got that fat Quaker into office. This was going to be a year to remember.

Oh, I love how this new car smell. After I seal this next deal, I will be set for life.

"Can't this jalopy go any faster? You promised I would get to meet the president," the woman said in an annoying tone.

"The vice president."

"What?"

"I said you'd get to meet the vice president. They have invited us to dinner at the new Boardwalk Hall that is being unveiled tomorrow."

"Oh, well, then, I want to meet him. Don't fuck it up like the last time."

"Don't worry, Gladys, you're the star attraction at tonight's event," Midas said.

He turned his ring around so he could see the signet that helped him seal many deals. He considered it his lucky ring, and its gaze was all-knowing.

"Oh, what a pretty ring," Gladys said.

"This is my lucky signet. Ever since I came into contact with it, I've never lost a negotiation."

She took his hand and stared at the oblong curiosity.

"What the fuck?"

"What's wrong, my dear?"

"This ring... it winked at me."

"That's impossible. You must have had too many of those Gin Rickeys at lunch."

Midas smiled to himself. He knew full well the power of the ring and what it did to those who met its gaze. Tonight was to be a very special night indeed. Before he could finish the thought, the woman opened the passenger door. A gust of wind blew the door back. The woman giggled as she repeated the action. Her dress blew across her face, and Midas glimpsed her tiddles.

He licked his lips in anticipation as her flapping dress revealed her exposed private area. She took his hand and licked his fingers. A tingling sensation like no other overcame him. The vehicle swerved as he momentarily lost control.

"Stop, Gladys, we don't want to get into an accident now, do we?" Midas said.

The woman ignored him as she guided his ring finger deep within her. Midas slowed the vehicle to accommodate the extracurricular activity. The woman grasped his hand like she was possessed. She screamed, then a gust of chilly air peppered his face. He slammed the brakes as she tumbled onto the jagged rocks below. His signet ring winked at him. Its bloodshot gaze looked at him expectantly.

CHAPTER 2

Treeka's heart sank as massive explosions ripped through Manhattan. The buildings reverberated so violently that her teeth rattled. Screams of hundreds washed over her, like a torrent of water flowing over a gentle stream. The monster tossed her skinless cybernetic robots around like a kid's playthings. And there wasn't much of anything of her resistance left.

"Get out of there, Treeka," Jonny D said.

Aiko tugged her arm. "We need to leave—now!"

"Not without my father," Treeka said, falling next to the remains of Tsuyoshi Kiyomizu, her father.

"I got him," Mia said as she covered the remains with a makeshift blanket.

Treeka watched in horror as the hairy woman removed her sweater, then scooped up the remains of her father with her bare hands, before tying the bloody mess into a neat bundle.

"Treeka, let's go now," Aiko said.

"I suggest you listen to your young protégée. A hostile force is heading your way," Eliza, her AI, urged.

Treeka snapped out of her fog and into reality. It was like

she woke in a battle of flesh and despair. Everywhere she looked, there was carnage.

"There she is. The one who caused so much pain and destruction," a male voice said.

"Get her, before she gets away."

"I think we've worn out our welcome," Treeka said.

She ran like the wind. A quick glance behind her confirmed that Aiko was far behind her. She slowed her movement so the teen could catch up. Mia was holding off the crowd. She wielded a bus stop sign like it was a broadsword, braining anyone who got close. Treeka ducked into an alley. Aiko and Mia barricaded it with a dumpster. Aiko tried to reach a fire escape ladder, but came up short. The roar of the mob slammed against the dumpster. Mia groaned as the dumpster moved. The woman was strong, but the crowd was too many for one cybernetic warrior.

"Eliza, activate a jump on my mark," Treeka said.

Treeka ran toward the fire escape and ladder that ensured freedom. It was twenty feet off the ground. She used her cybernetic legs to propel her toward the fire escape. She slammed against the ladder. It was locked, but Treeka crushed the padlock in one hand like it was made of paper. The ladder rattled as it slammed against the pavement below. Seconds later, Aiko joined her. Mia wasn't so lucky. She got caught up in the crowd's frenzy. Someone smashed a glass bottle over her head. Blood oozed over her face. She screamed as another plunged a knife into her gut. One man scaled the ladder. Treeka punched the man so hard she nearly took his head off.

"We didn't cause this," Treeka said.

"Boombally boonuka," another man said.

"Hopsey duna," a child screamed.

Some people attacking Mia started biting; others punched,

stabbed, and pulled. One crazed-looking bald man bit her neck. Fresh blood oozed. He lapped it up like a thirsty dog.

What the fuck is the matter with these people?

Treeka and Aiko pulled up the ladder and secured it. Gunshots rang out and a white fiery blast of searing pain overwhelmed her senses. She diverted the pain sensors to dull the effect. But Aiko had no such defenses. They needed to leave this hellish chaotic mess and find out why these people were acting so strange.

"We've got trouble," Jonny D said over her communications link.

"What's the matter?" Treeka said.

"A chopper is hovering and spraying some green mist over the crowd."

"Is it making them crazy?" Aiko asked.

"Yes, they are acting erratically. How'd you know?"

"We have a bloodthirsty mob on our asses. Mia didn't make it."

Jonny D was silent for a long moment. "Mia was a good person. That bastard will pay for all the suffering he caused."

"He will, but first we have to survive. Meet us at the theater. We need to regroup."

"Affirmative, see you—"

The connection was severed.

"Come, we need to get the hell out of here. Soon the entire city will be after us," Treeka said.

Aiko nodded as the teen slit the throat of a crazed, half-naked man with what looked like a bloody rolling pin. He was naked from the waist down. The rest of his outfit resembled that of a cook. Other men leaped toward her like deranged frogs.

"Get that green goo on them," a man said, laughing.

Barrels dropped from a nearby building. Treeka had to

jump out of the way to avoid getting hit. The barrel exploded toward the men. They tried to run, but a shower of green goo hit them. They screamed as their skin vanished. Treeka could see the bone.

"You're hit," Aiko said.

Treeka looked down at her disintegrating right pinky finger.

"Warning! Imminent danger. Let no more radioactive fluid penetrate your armor. Exosuit integrity is at thirteen percent," Eliza said.

Treeka phased to avoid getting hit by any more goo. She scanned the area for the young ninja, but couldn't find any sign.

"Up here," Aiko said.

Treeka glimpsed Aiko scaling another fire escape. She ascended the nearest ladder and joined her young friend as they performed various parkour movements across the rooftops of the nearby brownstones. The streets were filled with what she called the impaired, people with no apparent control over their actions. Treeka had seen nothing like it. Some of the affected acted erratically, while others took more deliberate actions. It was as if these people were remote controlled.

"Over here," Aiko said as she flung herself atop another building.

Treeka followed and landed on the edge of the next building. It collapsed, and Treeka reached for the nearest object: an ancient-looking gargoyle.

"You will perish if you fall from this height," the AI chimed in.

Treeka glimpsed the ground, a cluster of impaired below. She reached up to get a better handhold. The stone gargoyle's head shattered. The slow, distant roll of what could only be gunshots echoed between the buildings.

Who is shooting at me?

As Treeka contemplated this, Aiko's hand came into view.

"Take it," the ninja said.

"Someone is shooting—"

Before Treeka could complete the sentence, a hot burning sensation shot up her hand.

"Danger. An unknown assailant is targeting you from a distance. Judging from the range, I estimate it to be fifty yards away. Your metacarpophalangeal joint has been severed in your fifth digit, or pinky finger," Eliza said.

Treeka watched in horror as the exosuit's effectiveness, along with her finger, evaporated. Aiko grabbed Treeka's forearm and pulled with both of her hands. Treeka's lifeblood made the effort difficult, but she was halfway over the ledge when more shots rang out. Chunks of stone exploded around them. Explosions of agony coursed through her left leg as she made it to the rooftop. The ninja dragged her behind an air conditioning unit. Bullets ricocheted as the shooter attempted to compensate for the new position. A pink milky liquid oozed from her hand. Aiko examined her body, then tore strips of her shirt, revealing bare skin. She formed a makeshift bandage over Treeka's right hand.

"Go easy or we won't have any shirt left," Treeka said, trying to make light of the situation.

"We need to get you real medical help. My makeshift patchwork will only go so far," Aiko said.

A nearby door providing access to the roof slammed open. A man dressed in black stood with a shield and a curved sword.

Who is that? Someone to finish us?

A spray of bullets rang out over the rooftop. Treeka heard the tinny sound of clanking metal around her. The man with the shield moved in their direction, holding the shield in front of him. The bullets stopped.

"Come, while they are reloading," the man said.

Treeka glanced at the man. He was tall, lean, and muscular

and wore the garb of a Japanese warrior. His face was covered in a battle mask that reminded her of a devil. Treeka's father had one, and she thought it was called a *Mempo*, the mask of a Samurai.

There's more than one of them?

With the aid of Aiko, Treeka limped toward the door that the mysterious man had exited. He covered them as they escaped into a darkened stairwell. Treeka wondered who this man was and who might have sent him. Pain shot through her hand and backside as she descended deeper into the darkness below.

"Who are you?" Aiko asked.

"The name's Sumoto. I'm a friend of your uncle's. Enough chit-chat. Your friend has lost a lot of fluid. And I have friends in the underground who can help, so let's roll," the man said.

Treeka drifted in and out of consciousness. She couldn't tell how long it had been since she had been shot. She remembered entering a basement, then going through a hidden entrance. Then the next memory was lying on a makeshift operating table. A doctor was operating on her. She didn't know who it was, but she hadn't given her permission.

"What are you doing?"

Darkness...

Sometime later, Treeka awoke to an all-too-familiar feeling of pain. Aiko sat on the floor, her head resting on her knees. It looked like she was trying to sleep. A man dressed as an ancient warrior stood on the opposite side of the bed.

"How are you feeling?" the man asked.

"Better—the pain has reduced."

"Good. Hiroto would be sad if they had hurt the daughter of his best friend."

"So you work for Aiko's uncle?"

"Not exactly. We're business associates. We've worked

together in the past. It's more than that. We're friends."

The man appeared to be conflicted about his relationship with Hiroto. She suspected it was more than a casual friendship. His feelings for the man ran deep.

"How do you know Aiko's uncle?"

The man looked around. When he was satisfied that no one was listening, he continued. "I've known Hiroto Abiko for a long time. I was betrothed to his sister, Jane—but that was a long time ago."

"Aiko's mother?"

The man shifted his gaze downward like there was something more interesting on the floor. He glanced at Aiko, then leaned closer to Treeka.

"Few people know this, but I'm Aiko's godfather. I've been keeping a close watch on her since her mother was murdered."

Treeka realized she knew little about Aiko's past. She changed the subject.

"Who was the doctor that operated on me?"

"His name is Dr. Clemmant. He runs a secret free clinic in Alphabet City. He also dabbles in cybernetics."

"Doc Chop must not like the competition," Treeka said.

"He doesn't know about Clemmant. If he did, he would be in danger. At one time, the men were friends. But that ended when he got Doc Chop's wife away from him. But that was before... never mind, I've said too much."

"Before what?"

"Dr. Clemmant helped Dr. Javitts'—Doc Chop's real name —wife Martha escape his clutches. It was not until later that Martha died."

"That's terrible. No wonder Doc Chop hates him."

"The good doctor has all but forgotten about his wife. From what I hear, he's taken a new bride. Your sister Meeka, if I'm not mistaken."

Treeka flushed at the memory of Meeka clobbering barrels of radioactive juice and covering hundreds of innocent people with it. Then later, the drones gassing innocents on the streets as they fled the clutches of Doc Chop's meat beast.

"How do you know so much about me and my sister?" Treeka asked.

"You're sort of famous in the cybernetic underground. Doc Chop has enhanced many with his back alley clinic. He must have implanted some backdoor in their security, because on the night of the attack, these people joined his fight."

"Fight against whom?"

"Anyone who isn't working *with* Doc Chop is working against him. Hence the reason you are here."

As Treeka thought over recent events, it all made sense. The meat beast was a distraction from his real agenda—world domination. Or at least to take control of New York.

He must work with someone else, or even a group of people.

"How long has she been awake?" Aiko asked.

"Not long. I was just bringing her up to speed with what I learned about Doc Chop," Sumoto said.

"We need to strategize on how we're going to take the doctor down."

"I think you need to recover from that hole in your side," Aiko said.

"I feel better already. That doctor that Sumoto arranged fixed me right up."

"Allow me to find the best path forward. I have eyes and ears in the underground that can help us here."

Treeka smiled at her fearless companion. She hadn't known her long, but she couldn't have asked for a better ally. Her traitorous sister betrayed her and, after many attempts to reason with her, she remains under the mad doctor's spell.

CHAPTER 3

Detective McKean pulled up to the brownstone on the Upper East Side. His shift was almost over, and he was looking forward to spending some quality time with his wife. His job often put a strain on their marriage, and after nearly fifteen years he had given some serious thought to quitting. But being a cop was in his blood, and he couldn't think of doing anything else. Reports of a man threatening to kill a group of hostages with his bare hands had hit the 911 channel. The operator informed the police dispatch of a prank. Then more calls came in for the same disturbance. Two other cruisers were at the scene and had set up a perimeter. McKean pulled up behind one of the vehicles.

"What's the situation?" McKean asked as he exited the cruiser.

"A suspected enhanced man on the top floor of this complex has at least ten hostages. And he is threatening to kill another unless we get him to his doctor," a uniformed officer replied.

"His doctor? Is he hurt?"

"He doesn't look injured, and I don't know who this *doctor* is. We have snipers on the roof of a building with a line of sight into the penthouse where the assailant is holed up. According to the snipers, he is more than capable of fulfilling his promises. He threw a three-hundred pound victim to their death, with his bare hands."

"If he's not enhanced, then he's probably on drugs. We need to be prepared for anything," McKean said.

"The thought crossed our minds, but he is lucid. The snipers pulled up a heat map of the room and the man is half machine."

"I don't think I've seen that much metal in a man before—"

A window on an upper floor smashed outward as two more people came flying down.

"He's throwing victims out the window," the sniper said.

"If you have a clean shot, then take it," a man said.

Moments later, shots rang out and echoed between buildings.

"We got him," the sniper said.

"Who's the officer in charge?"

The uniformed cop pointed to a middle-aged man in a suit talking to someone on the radio.

"Detective McKean here. I heard the call on the radio. I think you could use a hand."

"Thanks for your offer, Detective, but I will have to decline. We have things well in hand here," Sargent Ramirez said.

News helicopters flew overhead, and people at the perimeter began to shout.

"I don't think you understand what you are dealing with," McKean said.

"Excuse me?" The sergeant turned on him, irate. "The hell I don't. Now get the hell out of my crime scene."

McKean sighed, returned to his car, got in, and started it. Before he could put it into gear, the uniformed officer waved to him. McKean rolled down the window so he could hear the officer.

"Hey, McKean, come here, will ya?"

The detective turned off the car and as he headed toward the officer, six more bodies landed on various police cars. The sniper opened up.

"The man won't die."

"Send in the team," Sargent Ramirez said.

"One hostage remains. The man is waving a white flag," a sniper said.

"Is he surrendering?"

"I'm not sure."

"Get two units up there. McKean, we can use your skills in there."

"Affirmative."

McKean followed a group of uniformed officers inside the building. The officers split up. Some took the stairs, but McKean and a group of officers took the elevator. When the officers emerged onto the penthouse floor, McKean took the lead. A body of a young woman was lying on the floor near the elevator–no pulse. Congealed blood was caked around the baseball-sized hole in the woman's chest. An explosion rocked the penthouse. The entire floor shook. Many of the officers lost their balance and fell to the floor. McKean and the uniformed cops hurried forward toward the only set of doors. After several kicks, the door gave way. A man stood near the right-side corner of the room. His tall features and long white hair reminded McKean of a college professor. Cries of anguish came from the corner. A young girl about ten years old was curled up in a ball.

"Stop or I'll kill her," said a man with his palms up toward the girl.

"Get down on your knees," McKean said.

The man raised his hands and thrust them in McKean's

direction; the man's arm was more metal than skin, and a soft blue radiance glowed in each hand. A crackling noise emitted from somewhere in the room. McKean could see cracks opening, forming in the walls and marble floor. The suspect pushed his arms forward and projectiles flung from his sleeve. The weapons exploded as they came into contact with an officer. McKean opened fire and emptied his piece into the enhanced man. He stumbled and fell. McKean rushed into the room. One hostage remained. The uniformed officers handcuffed the injured man and checked for weapons.

"The assailant is down, minor child in the room. Requesting medical personnel," an officer said over a radio.

"It's all right, dear. You're safe," McKean said.

The girl turned to face him. Her eyes were as black as pitch, no whites.

"What did he do to you?"

The girl covered her face with two dirty hands.

"It's okay. I'm here to help you," McKean said.

"Eight-seven-zero-four-nine-five, returning to the nest," the assailant said.

"Two-three-five-nine-eight-seven, protecting the gatekeeper," the girl said.

"What was that?" a uniformed officer said.

The two uniformed cops picked the man up. The metal in the man glowed with a blue-white light so bright it illuminated the room with the power of thousands of lumens. Before McKean could process the strange actions of his suspect and victim, the girl screamed. All glass in the penthouse and several windows of all the surrounding buildings were shattered. The officers and McKean dropped to the floor. His ears were filled with blood. The man and the girl walked out of the room as if they had all the time in the world. No additional opposition was given.

McKean's head was spinning and blood was dripping from his nose, ears, and mouth. Some of his teeth fell out.

What just happened?

Treeka strode into the kitchen where her spare nutrition cartridges were stored. She had less than 5 percent and was feeling the effects of her rapidly depleting source of energy. Aiko and Sumoto sat at a nearby table. A map of New York was stretched out before them. Several red X's were positioned at various points around the city. Treeka noticed a pattern. The X's were strategically placed. She didn't know what purpose they served, but if it had anything to do with Doc Chop's gas attacks, they needed more information before any counterattack would be possible.

Aiko called for her as she was replacing her cartridge.

"How does that make you feel?"

"What are you talking about?"

"Your energy source. Does it feel strange when you insert that into your body?"

"A little, but it makes me feel so much better once I do."

Treeka described an unpleasant situation when she ran out of the mixture that contained the amino acids and protein compounds. Her friend Junior ground sardines up to give her a boost. Her cybernetic stomach was far too small to process food like a human. She explained that the nutrition cartridges were necessary to keep her operational.

"That's fascinating, but what happens when you run out?"

"Nigel, a good friend of mine, has provided enough of the mixture to last a while. But eventually I will need to make some more."

Sumoto cleared his throat.

"Now that we're all here, I suggest we get down to business."

The hacker pointed to one of the X's. "Do you know what this is?"

"Attack points?"

"Close. They are infection points."

"What is that?" Treeka asked.

"Doc Chop has his drones positioned in spots around the city to infect the most people. According to my intel, the crazy son of a bitch has introduced a new threat in the form of human bombs."

"Exploding people? That sounds messy. Where has that happened? And how do you know about it?"

"Remember, I have eyes and ears everywhere."

If the doctor has started using people, then he has gone mad. And my sister is in the middle of it!

"The latest attack was on the Upper East Side last night. Two such bombs went off, and one of them was a little girl."

"That is sick," Aiko said.

"Yes, and the officer on the scene reported some unusual behavior from these individuals. A numbering and codeword system was used. Then the girl called the adult. She was with the gatekeeper."

"Any clue on what that means?"

"No, but I have my best code breakers working on the numbering system used."

"We need to take out these drones in a coordinated strike. If we have enough people, we can disable the entire system. Then when the doctor sends someone to fix it we can interrogate them for answers," Aiko said.

"I like it, but we might not have enough time. Doc Chop has already crippled the city's infrastructure and emergency services are scarce. Hell, even the police have left the city to the criminals."

"I can't stay here. I need to help the people while I can."

"Well, I'm not going to let you go alone. In case you have forgotten, there's someone trying to kill you."

Treeka placed a hand over her wounded area. Try as she might, she couldn't think of who the sniper was. Doc Chop wasn't the kind of man to keep snipers on the payroll. There was Nozomi, but she liked to dispatch her prey up close. She decided to go incognito and rig a disguise.

"I could change my appearance."

"I think we need more than just a cosmetic facelift. We need to make a complete change to your physique. I have men that can work some magic."

"The only person who can do that is Dr. Ash, my creator," Treeka said.

"Where can we find Dr. Ash?" Sumoto asked.

"I don't know if she would even return my calls. We didn't part on very good terms. What about using the doctor that fixed me?"

"I don't think he is available, but I wouldn't trust just anyone to perform such a delicate procedure. We wouldn't want to mar your beauty."

"I don't care about that; it's the people I want to save. As long as my crazy bitch sister is with that madman, I won't rest until they are taken down."

"Very well, take this and find Sister Grace in Alphabet City. She's one of the best cosmetic surgeons I know. But I think you should try to at least reach Dr. Ash," Sumoto said, handing her a card with a butcher knife design on it.

Treeka nodded. A wave of emotion overwhelmed her when she thought of her sister. She had brought her back from the grave only to have her ripped away by that fucking madman. As much as Treeka hated Dr. Ash, she feared that her team of defenders wasn't strong enough to even put a dent in Doc Chop's incursion, let alone defeat him. Unbeknownst to everyone, the doctor had been planning the fall of the city for a long time.

Where is that back door?

Treeka remembered Dr. Ash telling her about an emergency beacon to reach her creator. She was able to sift through her logs, which most people called memories. All of her experiences were saved in her neural network. She realized that most of her memories were unpleasant ones since waking on Dr. Ash's table almost a year ago. But there were plenty of good ones. Meeting Nigel and Aiko were some of the best in recent memory. She wondered where he was now. He was one of the few she'd ever met that wanted to help, instead of exploit her.

I need to work on some trust issues. Especially since Meeka betrayed me.

Moments later, she found the linkage back to Dr. Ash. It was a link that activated her communications system, but she visualized it as an ugly red button. To be used only in an emergency. She activated the link and a picture of the older doctor appeared before her. In the early stages of her awakening, she came to see Dr. Ash as an aunt. Someone who understood that blood was indeed more precious than water.

System Message: *The attempted call has failed. Please try again later.*

Treeka didn't know how her emergency communications system worked, but she assumed it connected to traditional technology like cellular communications systems. If that was the case, it would make sense that it was unavailable, since the city's infrastructure was failing. The attack of the meat beast had pushed the city over the edge.

Maybe I should wear a disguise?

She determined it was better to know who her enemies were now that someone was targeting her. A gleam of light shone through the window. She held her side as her wound gave her the painful reminder of her most recent attack.

I know you're out there, sister. I love you, even if I hate what you've become.

A ringing sound emanated throughout the room. The sound was akin to alarm bells at a fire station. Treeka turned toward the source of the noise. Sumoto stared at the phone like it was a viper.

"What's wrong?" Treeka asked.

"This is a landline that I've had for years."

"Okay, and so why don't you answer it?"

"This line never rings. I didn't think anyone even had the number."

Sumoto picked up the phone with the utmost care. It was like he was afraid to find who was on the other side.

"Hello... I see... Hold please," Sumoto said, handing the phone to Treeka.

She picked up the phone, trying to imagine who it might be. And how did they know to call her here?

"Identify yourself," Treeka said.

"Well, hello, Treeka. Is that any way to greet an old friend," a man's voice said.

Who is this? It can't be—Doc Chop?

"How can we be friends when I don't even recognize your voice!"

She heard the man let out a tired sigh. "It's your old pal Dr. Sylvester Javitts."

"Why don't you invite me over? I would like to do the city —and world—a favor by removing your head. It's my turn to punish you."

Treeka felt her face flush as the man laughed. "I can see where Meeka gets her temper from. Your sister misses you."

"So long as she's with you she's dead to me. What do you fucking want from me?" Treeka asked.

"I've come to a realization. I would rather have you as an ally, not an enemy. I think we can help each other."

"Do what? I'm not interested in taking over the city or harming others."

"You're a born assassin. You can't change who you are, not really."

"Even assassins have a code of honor. You exploit people for fun and profit. You're a fucking blight on the world. I look forward to putting you down like the mangy cur that you are."

"I thought you were smart. You should know that my team is in control of most of the city's infrastructure. Most of the politicians have already abandoned the city. Even the mayor gives press conferences from his residence in the Catskills. He doesn't even know what is going on. Much of the police force, the few that remain, are already on my payroll. I can pick you up at any time."

"I suggest you finish the job while you can."

"In respect for my new bride and your sister, I'm giving you one final opportunity. You will have the freedom to carry out the final solution."

"You make me sick. I'm going to feed your genitals to you before putting you down. But in the spirt of love I will give you one chance. Stop what you're doing and leave the city or stay and die. You have twenty-four hours to decide."

The line went dead. Treeka wondered how much of what he said was true. She decided it didn't matter because she had to rid the world of the most evil man she'd ever known.

CHAPTER 4

Enyo disembarked from her private jet and was careful not to step into any puddles that were forming on the tarmac of LaGuardia Airport in New York. The billowing smoke and sirens made for a horrific sight. This great city had fallen into urban chaos in a matter of months. Life was different in this land, and the failure of her most experienced agents had forced her presence. She hated traveling to America. The last time she had been here, some local gang members nearly dismembered her. She still saw the greedy look in the men's eyes every time she closed her eyes. Enyo touched a scar that traveled from her neck to her navel.

I had to mar my skin with a tattoo to hide that scar.

"We are almost ready for you, madam," a wide man in a suit said.

The thin Asian woman gave the man an appraising look, then gazed upon the orange-and-red sky.

"We are ready for extreme measures much earlier than expected."

"I have your elite crew on standby."

"Execute with extreme prejudice."

"I cannot guarantee we won't have any collateral damage."

"Very well. If that is the cost of taking care of our client's business, then it is acceptable."

The man nodded, then resumed his telephone conversation.

Enyo pulled up her cybernetic interface. While Sherman was activating the sleeper agents, she would need to ensure success in other ways. Two of her agents were in the middle of Manhattan, and she waited to reactivate them until the right moment.

Time to see where they are.

She selected the mapping interface and tapped the "Agent Awareness" option. She had to be careful when activating this, as they could trace the signal back, even with VPNs in place. Two dots were displayed on the map. One was near midtown; the other was downtown. She selected the dot in midtown and reviewed the dossier.

Name: *Anya Middleton*

Skills: *Martial Arts, expert in bladed combat.*

Seniority: Nine months of service.

WARNING: **Agent is related to the target. Exercise caution.**

This is an unexpected complication. Her loyalty must be tested.

Enyo pulled up Anya's service record. She had been taken into the Society at an early age, but at ten she was too old to begin any meaningful training. She recalled the girl's sprit. Her father abandoned her shortly after her mother disappeared.

"Delphina, please tell me why you suspect Anya is a blood relative of our target," Enyo asked.

After a moment, the AI responded with some cryptic information about the girl matching several correlations that made the AI suspicious.

"It is likely your young apprentice will not remember her

biological father. But the human mind has a funny way of reassociating connective patterns. I call this process connective tissue," the AI said.

"I will keep that in mind. Thank you, Delphina," Enyo said.

▭

Treeka was about to try Dr. Ash again when an encoded message appeared across her cybernetic interface.

System Message: *You have an incoming encrypted video message from an unknown recipient. Would you like me to play it now?*

"Yes, Eliza. Play it now."

An image of a woman in a kimono appeared. She was Asian and had the most perfect face she had ever seen.

No human has such exacting features.

"Hello, Echo-451. You don't know me, but I'm a fan. Your precision handling of that awful meat beast was most impressive and has earned you an audience with the Silent Assassins Society."

Nozomi spoke of this group—often!

Treeka paused the video as she tried to remember what the cruel cyborg had said. She remembered the group was an elite hit squad.

What does this group want with me?

Treeka restarted the message. The woman stared into the camera with purpose. She couldn't tell how old the woman was. Her features looked timeless. She might as well be staring at a statue.

"You may be wondering how to submit your audition. The answer is simple: you already have. Now keep up the good work and you shall hear from us again soon."

Who is this woman?

Moments later, the video message stopped and was replaced by a black screen.

I need to find out who she is. Has she contacted Meeka?

"Eliza, what is the source of the video message?"

"According to metadata, the message was sent from a local IP address, which I've tracked down to a building in Harlem. I've saved all the relevant details for your inbox."

A knocking sound came from the open door. Her gaze shifted. It was Sumoto. "Were you able to reach Dr. Ash?"

"No, but a strange message was sent to my cybernetic interface."

"What message? From whom?"

Treeka explained the contents of the message and gave a description to Sumoto. He rubbed his chin. He appeared to be conflicted. It was as if he was preparing to give her bad news.

"That sounds like Enyo. She runs the Silent Assassins Society, a mean group of cyborgs that eliminate problems for people, if the price is right."

"I'm not an assassin," Treeka said, disgusted.

She remembered her first job for Dr. Ash. She and Meeka killed several mobsters at Matzie's Karaoke Bar. She wasn't proud of what she had done. But she wasn't herself back then. Now, she had a new purpose.

"Even so, they rarely take no for an answer. We don't know who is targeting you, but having the Society on your side isn't a bad thing."

"I'm not joining a group of killers for protection. The shooter caught me off guard. That will not happen again."

Sumoto nodded. "Of course, I was not suggesting that you join. Only to keep all options open."

Treeka watched the samurai leave. She decided it was best

to keep her head down and her eyes open. She wasn't sure whom she could trust.

———

Dr. Sylvester Javitts examined the bank of monitors in his cramped office. The inch of dust and the smears on the windows reminded him that he had neglected his usual attention to detail. His recent experiment nearly backfired. The monster did its job a little too well. He didn't expect most of his clientele to evacuate the island so quickly. He expected to lose 30 percent of his cybernetic enhanced clients, not 90.

"There you are," a familiar female voice said.

"Hello, my dear. Are you ready for our next little experiment?" Dr. Sylvester said as he gazed into Meeka's eyes.

A look of doubt appeared on her face.

"Having second thoughts, sweetheart?"

"I'm not sure if I'm ready."

"Oh, but you are. You said so yourself. Besides, you know how important the plan is to our survival."

Meeka sat on the doctor's lap and gave him a passionate kiss.

"So, how do I get impregnated? Will little Sly be assisting?" Meeka said playfully.

Dr. Sylvester smiled. He couldn't help himself. If he pulled this off, his creations would live on forever.

"As much as I would love to, we need to be precise. Artificial insemination is our best option."

"Oh, I can't wait to be a mother. I will take that little itsy, bitsy thing to the store and the zoo. Maybe I will buy it a real monkey," Meeka said.

Dr. Sylvester smiled. She kissed him passionately again.

She's my kind of crazy.

"Don't get too attached. This is the first of many test runs we will need to make."

"My baby will be perfect the first time around. We have nine months to get a nursery ready. When do we start?"

"How about tonight?"

"Ooh, Sly. Tonight we shall make sweet love to celebrate our new arrival."

"Yes, dear—"

A loud ringing noise cut off the doctor. He picked up the receiver of a vintage rotary dial phone on his desk.

"Yes?"

"Hey, Doc; it's Rod. I've got a line on the girl."

Dr. Sylvester covered the phone with a hand.

"Would you excuse me, dear? I've got to take this."

Meeka winked.

"I've got to plan my baby shower anyway. See you tonight, lover boy!"

He waited for Meeka to leave his study.

"Sorry, Rodrick. What's the situation with that troublesome tramp?"

"I badly injured her. I was about to finish her off when some samurai came to her rescue. But I shot her in the gut with my sniper rifle. I also removed one of her digits. She won't be recovering any time soon."

"I need confirmation that she's dead. That bitch can be very resourceful. And she has a knack for getting people to follow her."

"I wouldn't concern yourself about it. But I will continue to watch the place."

"Yes, please do keep an eye on the place. I want to know if anyone comes to visit."

"Don't worry. I have a full surveillance package on her."

"See that you do," Dr. Sylvester said as he hung up.

He checked his notes on the serum. If his calculations were correct, the baby would be a toddler by the end of the day and a full-grown adult within a week. The child's brain capacity will exceed most human limitations. It would be a pleasure watching him grow to be a killing machine.

Just what every proud father needs.

The doctor leaned back in his chair and smiled. Everything was going to plan. The only loose end was that loose cannon of a cyborg.

Soon she won't even be able to stop what I have set in motion.

CHAPTER 5

THE BURNING SKYLINE of New York raged on as Nozomi watched. The monster had spread its dominion of chaos throughout the city, and the doctor reigned supreme. It was amazing how fast the city deteriorated. It was almost if it had been waiting for an excuse to be torn apart. Rick, her cyborg lover, seemed to be distressed since the city's fall. For some reason, he couldn't seem to shake off the compulsion to find his son. She humored him—for now. Soon his usefulness would be over and she would need to dispose of him. But he would be useful in the coming days. She needed to get that fucking bomb out of her head—and fast. A slamming sound broke her concentration.

"It's complete chaos out there," Rick said.

"Did you make contact?"

"Yes, your friend Malcolm put me in touch with another doctor who can remove the bomb."

"We need to be careful. If Doc Chop suspects something, he will flip that switch and we won't need to worry about anything ever again."

Rick put a hand on Nozomi's shoulder and kissed her forehead.

"I won't let that happen, babe."

No, but I would *let it happen to you in a heartbeat, lover.*

"For now, we should check in with the doctor."

"Yeah, it's been twelve hours, and he does have that thirteen-hour rule."

"Yeah, that fucker is still pulling the strings for now. But after I'm done with him, he will feast on his own entrails," Nozomi said.

Rick gave Nozomi a worried look.

"Don't worry, lover. I'm not going to go wild again."

"You can have your fun after we get these bombs out of our heads."

Nozomi gave Rick a wicked smile. "You can count on that. Now, let's see what that fucking doctor wants now."

———

An incessant banging sound emanated from the small apartment. A familiar faint light illuminated the small window. Anya leaped out of bed and crouched in the corner that provided the most protection while giving her the best tactical advantage. The door splintered and caved in, and a gigantic man strode into the room.

"Do you think you are ready for your first solo mission?" the man said while surveying the room.

Anya struck the man in the temple. While he stumbled, she took full advantage of the moment and poked him in the eyes. The man let out a scream and fell back into the ruined door frame. He swung at her, but missed. She spotted her sword on the wall. It was twenty feet away, but the man blocked her path, writhing from the pain in his malfunctioning eyeball. He grabbed one of her arms and twisted it behind her back. Her arm was pulsating with white-hot fury as the man held on.

Using her free arm, she grabbed a handful of the man's manhood and squeezed. He let out a high-pitched screeching noise. As he doubled over in pain, Anya punched him in the stomach.

Those training dummy exercises finally paid off.

The man groaned in agony and finally let go of her arm. She finished the job with a kick to the solar plexus. The man hit the floor so hard she thought she heard a crack.

Oh, my god... Did I... just kill Agent Six?

Anya checked the man's condition. His breathing was labored but constant. A growing crowd gathered outside Anya's apartment.

"I called the police," an older voice said.

"It's okay. My boyfriend and I were just fighting," Anya lied.

"That's one hell of a fight," an old bald man with stained pajamas said.

Anya tried closing the door, but it became stuck a few inches from the door frame.

Is this guy from the Society?

She kicked the door, and it slammed, inches away from the old neighbor's face. It wouldn't lock, so she wedged a chair to prevent prying eyes.

I'd better get this guy out of here before the cops come.

She filled a pitcher with water, rummaged in the freezer, then dumped the contents of all the ice trays she could find. Soon the water was frigid to the touch. She poured the cold water over the man's head. He tried kicking her, but she dodged the blows. Moments later, the tip of her sword was pressed against the assailant's neck. A drop of blood formed where the blade cut into the skin.

"Who are you?"

The man smiled.

Sirens blared in the distance and were getting closer.

"I don't know. Why don't you tell me," the man said.

Anya detected a hint of smug satisfaction in the man's voice.

He's taunting me!

"Fine, you can explain it to the cops. The old man down the hall called them."

"We have the police on our payroll. It will mean nothing to me, but you will be exposed. Are you sure you want to take the risk?"

"What do you want?" Anya asked.

"In my coat pocket," the man said.

Anya couldn't reach the man's pockets without losing her advantage.

"Empty your pockets."

She kept a watchful eye on the assailant as he removed a picture from his pocket. She snatched it from the man's hand. A woman about her age appeared in the photo. She was Asian and had black hair with purple highlights.

She's the one who fought that meat monster!

"What's this?" Anya asked.

"Your first assignment," the man said.

"Impossible. This is not the target I decoded."

"Let's just say that assignment is the main course, and I've just served up the appetizer. Either can be finished without the other, but together they make it complete."

This man speaks in riddles and it's all part of the initiation. Challenge accepted, motherfucker!

Anya's eyes shifted back to the picture; moments later she dodged the man's foot. She got into a dragon stance and prepared to defend her ground. The sirens stopped just outside the building.

"You have a choice: you can fight me and explain to the

police why a waitress from Hell's Kitchen is wielding an ancient Katana that is worth more than she makes in five years. Or you can accept your first solo mission. The choice is yours."

She heard men climbing the stairs and estimated she had fewer than thirty seconds before they were at the door.

"I accept the mission."

"Next time, I will kill you, bitch," the man said as he fled through the fire escape.

She watched as he shot a grappling hook and scaled a nearby building with ease. She already had the story ready for the police. An abusive boyfriend came by to rough her up a little.

"Open up, it's the police."

Time for your award-winning performance, Ayna; now make it a good one.

The bruising from the altercation she'd just had with the Society's messenger would back her story. She loved the excitement her real job provided, but grew wary of the stories she had to invent to protect her cover. She marveled at her ability to convince even the most skeptical. With a little preparation she could play any part and tonight she delivered her most convincing performance to date.

CHAPTER 6

Midas Mink sat at the end of the terrace. His wheelchair made it difficult to see the entire skyline, but he could make out much of the flatiron district well enough. His hedge against the mayor of New York had paid off. The monster that had terrorized Midtown Manhattan was good for business. Many police officers quit after the incident due to lack of pay, a hiring strike, and an unprecedented 18 percent tax hike; many people fled the city. Many of them had abandoned their mortgages and took what they could carry. The foreclosure rate on Manhattan Island was approaching 40 percent. Bums and other gutter-trash took up residence in some of the less guarded empty brownstones. The residents who stayed and could afford it hired armed guards. Many less fortunate had to take their chances on the street.

I think I will add a new tier of protective services. Everyone will need protection soon.

A buzzing sound emanated from the apartment. It sounded weak, like a dying animal.

"Will you please answer that, Jonas?" Midas said.

"I'm sorry, sir. I was a bit preoccupied with ordering your

weekly supply of food. It takes significantly longer to order even the most basic of necessities these days."

Jonas is getting too old to help with my daily needs. I think I will get a younger, prettier assistant. One who doesn't mind taking care of my other human needs.

Midas smiled at the thought. The channel one news blared throughout the apartment. Stories of infrastructure decay and carnage from the resulting collapse were all over the news these days. Midas benefited from the chaos more than others, but he was always looking for other opportunities to diversify.

"Your companionship for the evening has arrived, sir. She is waiting for you in the master suite."

"Excellent. Thank you, Jonas."

His servant lowered a tray he was holding. He took the glass of water and a blue pill from the tray.

"Have you received the financials from our investment in that clinic in Hell's Kitchen?" Midas asked as he put the empty glass back on the tray.

"No, sir. Dr. Sylvester promised a courier, but they are long overdue. I will contact the doctor first thing in the morning. But for now just enjoy your companionship that I have arranged."

Midas nodded as he maneuvered the small wheelchair to the master suite where his young companion waited.

▭

Treeka refilled her nutrition cartridge based on the instructions Nigel had left for her. It was a messy business, but she eventually got it refilled. After checking her fluid levels and having Eliza run a full diagnostic, she strode to the window and took a handful of curtain. She desperately wanted to see sunlight again. Spring was almost here and she had only seen the darkening of clouds on the horizon. She flung the curtain back: water ran across the window. She closed her eyes and tried accessing another memory from her childhood. She'd grown up in Los Angeles and couldn't remember how many rainy days she'd had to contend with. Gray clouds with a greenish tint covered the sky far into the horizon. There would be no sunny days here. Doc Chop had put a stop to that when he gas bombed the city.

"It gets better with the rain. The gas isn't as effective," a man's voice said.

Treeka shot a glance in the direction of the voice. Sumoto stood just behind her.

"I need to put a stop to this madness," Treeka said.

"I have been doing some thinking. Please hear me out before saying no."

Treeka gave him a curious look.

"Doc Chop has too much of a foothold in the city. There's little we can do alone. We need help," Sumoto said.

"How many of the local forty-five do we have?"

Sumoto gave her a confused look.

"Jonny D's men?"

"Yes."

"You're a local hero among the working class in Queens."

"All I tried to do was eliminate a mad doctor."

"You did more than that. Nobody had ever challenged Doc Chop before. He may have seemed like a decent guy when the workers had opted to become one of his cybernetically enhanced. But when the work dried up and the payments came due, he repo'd the implants and made a bloody mess doing it."

"I had no idea," Treeka said.

"Well, those workers are still looking for their pound of flesh, so you will probably be able to get some fresh recruits, but precious few of them remain. I propose an alliance with a new group."

"With whom?"

"I believe you have been in contact with the leader. Her name is Enyo."

Treeka watched the rain dance across the window. The city was going to have many dreary days if Doc Chop had his way.

"I will agree to a meet; if I like what I see, then we can discuss alliances."

"That sounds reasonable. I will set something up."

Treeka hated the thought of getting entrenched with a hit squad, but they had the power to eliminate Doc Chop for good this time.

With the assistance of his wheelchair, Midas glided into the room. His companion waited for him on the bed, wearing little more than a skimpy negligee that showed a generous amount of her skin.

I bet she's enhanced in every area that matters.

Midas smiled.

"What's your name, sweetheart?"

She opened her almond-shaped eyes and smiled.

"SoMay," the woman said as she sat on her knees in the middle of the bed. Midas's breath caught in his throat.

"This is for you," she said, sliding off the bed to hand him an envelope.

She's so beautiful. I feel the effects of that blue devil now.

He took the envelope and opened it. A hand-written note on thick parchment displayed an elegant script he had not seen in a long time.

Dear Midas,

Please accept my gift. SoMay will provide you with much

companionship and has an increased sexual appetite. She loves older men, so I hope you approve.

Yours truly,

Dr. Sylvester Javitts

Midas hoisted himself out of the wheelchair and onto the bed, and removed his robe. SoMay snuggled next to him and stroked his hardening shaft.

"You know what to do," Midas said, and she removed his underwear. In an instant, she was naked and mounting the older man. She rode him mercilessly. He suckled on her breasts as he burrowed deep inside her.

About thirty minutes later, the old man was lying sweaty and naked on his silk sheets. His companion was as perfect as ever. Despite their intense lovemaking, the woman had not even broken a sweat. He caressed her long, black hair and put his hands on her body. She was warm to the touch, but didn't feel like a real woman. Her skin was a bit off. It didn't feel as smooth as many of the woman he'd had over the years. Her breasts and thighs felt real enough, but other parts of her body had a rubbery feel. She had given him some of the best sex he had in years, and he wanted more. He was about to attempt to mount her when his girth shrank. His pole was at half-mast and he doubted if he could perform for the rest of the evening. He decided to strike up a conversation. He had never had any meaningful discussions with a sex robot before, but maybe she would be different.

"Thank you for a wonderful evening, my dear. I would like to know where you're from."

The woman gave him a confused look.

"I'm from the clinic. Didn't the note give you the information that you require?"

"It did indeed."

The woman gazed upon his rapidly shrinking penis. Is

there anything else I can do for you while we wait for your recharge?

"No, we might be waiting for some time before that happens. Let's go to sleep."

SoMay helped him under the covers and she cuddled next to him as he drifted into a dreamless slumber.

CHAPTER 7

Treeka cringed as she examined the holes in her exosuit. She determined that the suit was too badly damaged for her. She said a silent thank you to Dr. Clemmant, the mystery man who had extended her expiry date. At least until the next skirmish on the battle zone that was the streets of New York.

"I'm going with you!" Aiko said.

"You should take care of your uncle. I will be fine."

Treeka didn't know if that was true, but her optimistic nature wanted to believe the lie. The truth was, after her near miss on the rooftop, she wasn't as confident as she wanted others to believe.

I need to take down the doctor before he becomes too strong. Hell, who am I kidding? He already is too strong. But I have to try. Even if it kills me.

Aiko shot her an apprehensive glance.

"Once Sumoto's surgeon gets finished, no one will recognize me. Not even my own sister."

"Tell you what. I will check on Uncle, then I will see you after your facelift."

"Deal, we will meet back here in forty-eight hours."

"I'm going to hold you to that," Aiko said.

Treeka gave the ninja a hug.

"We will meet again—little sister."

Treeka waited until Aiko was well on her way before she dared to move.

Two hours later

Treeka made some makeshift repairs on the exosuit. She had no idea if it would hold up if someone started shooting at her, but she wasn't doing any good sitting on her hands waiting for the doctor. She checked the clips for one of the handguns. She lost track of how many times she had unloaded, then reloaded, the weapon.

Time for action.

Treeka exited into the alley as rain poured across her body. It was a refreshing reminder that she was still alive. When she was a girl she'd always enjoyed rainy days. She especially liked how the water washed away the filth that seemed to invade her life. Treeka adjusted her hoodie, then headed toward the train. She heard a chirping sound and activated her neural communications link. She didn't want to attract unwanted attention by talking out loud to herself. She glanced at the caller identification and the only identifiable indicator was that it was from a New York location. She answered the link and an older woman with many implants filled her display.

"Sumoto said you'd be coming in hot. Take the Avenue B entrance off the alley. I will know you're close and meet you."

The video cut off as soon as the woman's last sentence was finished. Moments later she was riding a southbound R train toward downtown. She detected some stares from some people in the crowd. A child with a toy, a bald man pretending to read a newspaper. An old man sitting on a bench. Everyone seemed to be watching her. A diagnostic check revealed that she was at 71 percent combat efficiency. She knew it was wise to rest, but she didn't have another day to rest. Doc Chop had put something big into motion, and she needed to stop it.

Stop being paranoid. These people are not out to get you.

"Eliza, do you detect any threats in the immediate area?" Treeka said.

"None detected, but I do sense something, so be on guard."

"Can you be more specific?"

"Data from the city and metro camera systems suggest that a tall figure in a raincoat has taken the same route as you. There has been no aggressive moment, but I will continue to monitor."

The train rocked as it sped up between stations. The lights flickered erratically, and she readied herself for an attack. She took a seat at the back of the train. If she was going to crack a few skulls, she didn't want any civilians to get caught in the crossfire.

"Mind the right side of your body or your fleshy side. You're still injured and it won't take much for the stitches to rip. Your regeneration systems are working, but only at seventy-five percent," Eliza said.

"Approaching Twenty-third Street. This is the Brooklyn-bound Broadway local," a muffled voice announced.

One more stop, then I transfer to the L.

She waited until the train was about to depart the Fourteenth Street station and nearly got the door slammed on her. She found the Brooklyn-bound L train stop, then casually leaned against a wall. She didn't see anything out of the ordinary. Eliza didn't, either. Moments later the L train came into view. She scrutinized each passenger as they departed the train. When she was satisfied that no one was going to attack, she stood near the rear of the car. After an underground incident in a similar train car, she loathed being on or near trains. But since she didn't want to attract attention to herself, she reasoned it was the best and quickest form of transportation available. Especially in the rain. When the train arrived at the First Avenue station at East Fourteenth Street, Treeka spotted a rough-looking man with salt-and-pepper hair and a long battered face. It looked like the man had been in a fight with a legion of alley cats. He starred at Treeka for longer than she was comfortable. She bolted as the door was about to close.

"DANGER," Eliza said.

Her AI's voice reverberated throughout her skull. Treeka watched in horror as the man yanked the sliding doors apart and stepped off the moving train. The motion propelled the man into a concrete column. The tiles shattered from the man's girth. Treeka got into a defensive stance. She dodged a punch, then kicked him in the solar plexus. He stumbled and grunted, but kept coming.

"You need to keep him off your right side."

The man was nimble for his size, and he danced around her with the efficiency of a ninja. She was having a difficult time avoiding all of his blows. He positioned his fingers into a claw and struck her vulnerable side. She was blinded by a searing pain so intense that she was temporarily incapacitated. She fell to her knees as she grasped her side. Screams from people ensued. She blinked sweat and tears from her eyes as she recovered. A group of men took her attacker. She watched in horror as the brute dislocated one man's arm, then kicked his unresponsive carcass across the platform. Another man got his neck broken for his trouble. The remaining men ran.

"I'm going to crush you," the man said.

He clenched his fist and ran toward her.

"You're in no condition to fight. Bracing for impact, activating hard-shell mode," Eliza said.

Treeka's skin turned into a hard, stonelike substance; she

closed her eyes as the man bore down on her. A moment later she opened her eyes to find the man gasping at his throat. He made several wet, low guttural sounds, then his head slid off his neck and onto the floor. Behind the man was a tall female figure dressed in a red and silver outfit. A mask with a creature engraved on it hid the newcomer's face. She put away her sword, then reached for Treeka.

"I'm a friend; come with me. You're in no condition to fight."

"Who are you?"

"My name is Anya. We need to move before reinforcements come."

"I'd listen to her. Two highly electrified individuals are headed your way," Eliza said.

The armor made moving difficult. She accepted the masked woman's hand, and a moment later she was back on her feet. Two slender figures strode onto the platform, and they had a glow about them.

These people seem familiar.

Treeka noticed that the figures appeared to be a male and female version of the same person or body type. They could have been brother and sister, but Treeka guessed they were manufactured in a lab. She felt the small hairs on her neck rise as the air electrified.

"Let's go! The Voss twins will fry us where we stand," Anya said.

"The tall one knows of us," the male figure said.

"Yes, after that show we made at city hall, everyone knows who Edgewick and Sylvana are," the female figure said.

The twins slapped their hands together. Treeka and Anya were propelled into a nearby wall.

"Regeneration system at forty percent and dropping," Eliza warned.

The lights in the station went out as the twins readied an electric ball. Moments later it shot toward them. Anya reached for something at her belt as the ball of electricity threatened to finish them off. A translucent shield enveloped them in a bubble. Bolts of electricity showered over them.

"We can't take much more of this," Anya said.

As the electricity faded, the twins put their hands together. A white light formed and shined out between their fingers. Treeka rummaged through her utility belt looking for anything she could use as a weapon. She'd exhausted her supply of throwing knives, but she found her phasing bracelet. The device allowed her to travel several blocks at a time. The limitation was line of sight. While she had no clear escape route, she decided to think of an offensive use. The white light formed into a gigantic sphere. She put the bracelet on her wrist.

"Drop the shield."

As Anya complied, Treeka twisted the bracelet and teleported herself into the nearest twin. Her father had warned her not to teleport herself into an inanimate object or bystander. The effects were deadly; the male twin exploded. Chunks of meat and blood covered the immediate area. Treeka un-phased and plunged a dagger into the female twin's heart. The woman gave Treeka a look of surprise and confusion. Bolts of electricity shot through Treeka, then stopped as the woman expired.

"Well done! Welcome to the Silent Assassins Society," Anya said.

Treeka's vision faded as someone slipped a black bag over her head from behind. She tried to resist, but in her weakened state she was easily overpowered. Something pinched the fleshy part of her right arm.

"Eliza, what's happening?"

Her AI answered, but the response was muffled. It sounded like someone speaking underwater.

What was in that—

Moments later she collapsed in a heap on the floor.

———

Later that evening Treeka woke on a soft bed. The sheets felt soft to the touch, like silk.

"Eliza, are you online?"

The silence was deafening. All sensory input was unavailable. It was like someone shut off her audio. She couldn't even hear herself speak. The room was darkened, but she could make out vague outlines of the bed and other objects in the room. The temperature was neither too hot nor cold. Despite being naked she wasn't uncomfortable. She sat up in the bed, and was treated to a magnificent view of Manhattan. From her vantage point, panoramic views of the city lay below. The view reminded her of eating in a fancy restaurant with a revolving top floor. Her parents used to take her and Meeka to a place called the Top of Nine in Westwood. She didn't remember the place for its food, but for the ambiance. The memory conjured up the joyful past, but they cut into Treeka like a sharp knife. She knew she could never revisit that time or replicate her joy. Her future contained only heartbreak and despair.

"How are you feeling?" a female voice asked.

She couldn't find the source of the voice. A dreadful thought came to mind: *Someone is watching me. Like an animal in the zoo.*

"Who are you? Show yourself!"

"My name is Enyo, and I run a very special group of talented individuals."

"Did you kidnap them, too?"

"I'm sorry for the black bag operation, but I had to be sure you were the real Tomiju Kiyomizu."

"My name is Treeka!"

"Forgive me, child, but we have little time. I believe we are on the same side."

"Same side of what? Stop toying with me. If you are on my side, then I demand to see you in person."

A moment later a door opened to her right. Harsh white light poured in. Treeka recognized the outline of the person she saw in the video.

"It was not my intention to kidnap or coerce you in any way. The city is out of time and I know you care about the people. One of our mutual friends told me as much."

Enyo held out her palm, and an image of Nigel Watson appeared.

Treeka gave Enyo a hopeful look.

"You know Nigel?"

"Yes, Mr. Watson fights for our cause."

Enyo's olive complexion was smooth and her face was beautiful. But she seemed—artificial. The kimono was black, but the edges lit up as she spoke. Like the events in her life in recent times the woman's appearance seemed unreal. It was like she was living in a movie.

Time to see how much she really knows.

"When you say the city is in danger, can you be more specific?" Treeka said.

A frown formed on Enyo's face.

"Your distrust is understandable, but I will prove to you that we are on the same side. Ask me anything, and I will answer truthfully."

Enyo waved. Treeka's cybernetic interface came alive."

"Treeka! You're alive," Eliza said.

"I've reactivated your verification system. Your AI will verify my answers."

"You say we have a common enemy. Who is it?"

"The enemy is not one, but many. A cabal of highly resourceful and infinitely powerful enemies stands against us. One of these foes is Dr. Sylvester Javitts, you know him as Doc Chop," Enyo said.

"How many is he working with?"

"At least three other organizations with many criminal ties that span the globe. Doc Chop may want to take over Manhattan, but these accomplices want the world."

A chill went through Treeka like a dagger made of ice. She never knew anyone as devious or cunning as Doc Chop. Having others join Doc Chop's murderous tribe was unfathomable and distressing. She remembered Nigel discussing the cabal and it gave her hope to learn that people like Nigel were fighting for her cause.

"What evil exists in your ranks?"

Enyo seemed surprised by the question and seemed to be considering her next words.

"Yes, our group is not perfect. Years ago we accepted anyone who would suit our needs. And when I took over we were a professional hit squad. Now we take jobs that will improve society. We tend to do it in secret with no trace left behind. I have personally expelled all who contradicted our new mission. And, I believe you know one of them."

"Who?"

"You know her as Nozomi. She's also known as Noz the Dark."

Eliza, can you confirm any of this? Treeka said telepathically.

Yes, she is telling the truth. But she has her own agenda and needs you to end someone. She just hasn't brought that up yet, Eliza replied.

"Okay, I'm convinced that you're not completely evil, but what do you really want?"

A smile widened Enyo's narrow face. The sight was unnerving.

"I want to help you eliminate Doc Chop. I'm willing to give you the resources to do so, but I must ask for something in return."

Here it comes, no one does anything for free. She has an angle.

"And, what is that?"

"I need you, Treeka. All of you! I won't be satisfied with your membership. I want your heart, body, mind, and soul."

"What's so special about me?"

"You've been through more hardship than most people have experienced in several lifetimes. You are genuine and that is a rare gift."

Since her rebirth Treeka could think of little joy in her life. She briefly had it when her sister came back to her. Then later, when she realized she cared for Junior. But that all seemed like a very long time ago. If she could give herself over to something greater, it might give her the first joyful experience since childhood. She could think of only a few truly selfless people in her entire life: her father, Nigel Watson, and Aiko.

"I agree, but if I find that you are lying to me, I will hack you to bits."

"We will do great things together. Now follow me to the assimilation chamber."

"Wait, what is that?"

"I can't have you in your current form. I need to absorb your core. Your physical form will cease to exist, but you will not need it since you will be part of the Enyo construct."

"Enyo is not a person, I mean an individual?"

"I am made of many worthy souls and only select the most true of heart. It's better to show, rather than tell."

Enyo glided over to her position. She caressed Treeka's

face. A warm arousal overwhelmed Treeka. She wanted to be taken by this feeling and never let go. Her mind struggled to fathom what she was being asked to do. Her body wanted to be taken into whatever construct Enyo would give. Enyo kissed her gently upon the lips. Visions of righteous people solving impossible problems entered her mind. For the first time in perhaps a very long time, Treeka was at peace.

CHAPTER 8

Nozomi entered the underground lair of Doc Chop. She was unsure if she was going to find a suitable body double, but she was determined to get that dammed bomb out of her head by any means necessary. During her research, she'd discovered that Dr. Ash had left a programmable interface open for expansion. To Nozomi's surprise, she found instructions on transferring her consciousness to another host.

If I can't get this fucking bomb out of my body, then I will need to move my core to another body.

"Are you ready, lover?" Nozomi asked.

Rick nodded. "I will stand guard, but will I even recognize you once you've finished?"

Nozomi gave him a thoughtful look and responded by giving him the best kiss of his life, or at least she'd hoped it would be. She doubted that she would do the same after the procedure. Based on the information gathered from Dr. Ash's archive, she would be able to transfer her consciousness into another host. There were risks, but she was prepared to take them. Anything was better than waiting for the ticking time bomb to explode her head like a watermelon hit with a sledgehammer.

"I will need no more than an hour to complete the procedure. Ensure that nobody interrupts the procedure if you want me to take this body again."

Nozomi emphasized the point by taking his hand and moving it to one of her breasts. Rick's demeanor changed from a worried husband to a lustful teenager. He tried saying something, but she closed the chamber door before he could get the words out.

"Beatrice, ready my cybernetic firewall for the following exceptions: 80P9, H673, 586X, and 846R."

"These constructs are compatible and will be readied per your specifications. However, I cannot guarantee that your original cybernetic frame may be compatible with your new form."

Nozomi thought of all the times she'd used her beauty to get what she most desired. But now that she experienced what most would consider true love, she no longer cared.

"I accept the risks. Now tell me what my options are."

Beatrice filled her heads-up display with a myriad of options available from Doc Chop's inventory. She estimated there were at least sixty-four combinations of possibilities. She chose a torso similar to her original cybernetic frame. The breasts were perfectly symmetrical, but the skin appeared rubbery and as white as a store mannequin. She frowned at the lack of symmetry of her nipples. One was much larger than the other, but she told herself that she would find a way to regain control of her original body.

I'm going to look different, but I can use that to my advantage.

The appendages she had to choose from were limited to several skin pigments. While she could find the same body composition from the parts available, she couldn't find enough of the body type to match. She settled on a mix of skin shades and colors. Her left arm was ebony and her right was as white as snow. Her legs were an olive complexion. She reasoned that the symmetry and strength of her new body was more important than its looks. She needed to get revenge on a great many people and, thanks to her new body, she would have the element of surprise. She chose a pretty face. It was her experience that men were easier to control if they had something nice to admire.

"The chosen construct appears stable. The final stages of the transference process will require your consciousness to be transferred to the new body. I must stress that the procedure must not be interrupted."

Nozomi accepted and confirmed the final transference confirmation. The world faded as her rebirth took hold.

About an hour later, Nozomi finished adding the remaining cosmetic features. The procedure was completed, and Rick would be the first to see her rebirth. She examined her new shell. Despite its lack of uniformity, it was more flexible and seemed more durable than her previous body. She opened the door to the chamber and expected to see Rick. Instead, and to her surprise, Doc Chop stood before her.

"I see that someone has been a naughty girl. The transference chamber was not meant for you."

Unseen hands grasped her newly attached arms and legs. She snatched a glance at her captors and what she saw took her breath away. Dozens of tiny hands carried her away.

Midas contemplated the many years of wear and tear that he had put on his current body. He watched the choppy seas from his perch on the penthouse floor of the city's Edge Hotel. He could have chosen better hotels for his East Coast base of operations, but this one was unique because it was built at the end of the bluff just down the shore from Atlantic City. One of his favorite guilty pleasures.

It's been a good run, old boy. You've conquered your share of the fairer sex in your day. Now it's time for many more exploits.

A rapid knocking sound took him out of his thoughts. He opened the door and an attractive Asian woman answered. He had seen her before with his friend Dr. Javitts. It looked like she'd put on twenty pounds. He had seen a pregnant woman before, but the sight of this one was different because the additional body fat that most woman had during pregnancy wasn't as evenly distributed. The right side of her body looked normal, but her left didn't seem to carry any fat at all.

"Sly told me to fetch you," the woman said.

"What is your name, my dear?"

The woman gave him a distrustful glare.

"My name is Meeka. May I suggest that you get moving—before I shove my pregnant foot up your old ass?"

Midas grinned.

I don't care how important you are to Javitts. You shall pay for your lack of respect, my dear.

"Just a moment while I fetch my things."

"No need," Meeka said, as she shoved her way in.

Midas watched in astonishment as the young pregnant woman rushed past him to fetch his suitcase. She picked it up as if it weighed nothing. He noticed that she was careful not to use her right arm. He followed her through the back staircase of the hotel. Trash and other debris were piled on each landing. A pungent odor assaulted his nostrils.

"I had no idea this back staircase was here," Midas said.

"This view is not so glamorous. No one cares if you're a big wheel down here," Meeka said.

Midas removed the glove covering his left hand. A massive ring with a bloodshot eyeball appeared. It followed Meeka's every move.

"Whoa, what the fuck is that?"

"It's the all-seeing eye, my dear," Midas said, smiling.

"Get that away from me. It creeps me out."

"You have nothing to worry about, from this bauble, that is."

"What does that mean?"

"Nothing, my dear. Aren't we supposed to be heading to my transference ceremony?"

"What? No, we are just visiting Sly. Now let's go already," Meeka said.

"Yes, we shall."

Midas twisted the edge of the ring, a crimson light shot from it. Two men grabbed Meeka from behind. She responded by backhanding the man, his lip split open, blood oozed from the wound.

"You're going to pay for that, bitch," the man said.

The other man punched Meeka in the stomach. She let out a wheezing sound.

"Don't kill her. Not yet, anyway. We need to transfer into her little bundle of joy," Midas said, cackling.

"You're fucking crazy. Sly will not do that to me!"

"Who said that Dr. Javitts will have anything to do with the operation? You don't live almost a hundred years without taking certain precautions."

"What does that mean? Get off me!"

"Careful, boys, don't hurt my mother—not yet, anyway."

One of the men put a cloth over Meeka's mouth. She

squirmed for a moment before succumbing to the inevitable blackness of unconsciousness.

▭

Dr. Phil Clemmant pulled up to the brownstone on the Upper East Side. The darkening sky and the sight of smoke on the horizon put several unpleasant images in his mind. It had been ages since he had been to this side of town, and with the city in such disarray, he wanted to ensure his safety.

"Can you tell me more of my benefactor?" Clemmant asked.

"I can tell you that he has the means to pay for your sorry ass," the driver said.

Why is he so hostile?

The doctor reasoned that the private security detail from Queens and the armed driver were proof enough.

This job is going to set me up for life.

The view on Fifth Avenue was distressing. The high-end shops were rubble, like several explosions had gone off recently. As he rode across the bridge, several uncontrolled fires could be seen from upper and lower Manhattan. It was almost as if the police and fire departments walked away and left the city for the criminals. Just before leaving the bridge, a group of modern-day bridge trolls tried to collect from his driver. He responded by brandishing his .357 magnum. The creeps backed down. The car stopped at a modest, but surprisingly well-kept building, considering the mayhem in the city.

"This is your stop," the driver said.

"Are you going to escort me?"

"Nope, now get the hell out of my car."

The man waved the biggest handgun he had ever seen. A moment later, he pointed it at the doctor who got out.

I should ask for hazard pay, but this is the second lucrative job within a week. This is the last one, then I'm going to the Bahamas.

Phil admired the setting sun. Its radiance seemed to be tainted somehow. A group of youths strode toward him.

"Hey man, are you a doctor?" one of the youths asked.

"Why do you think I'm one?"

"Don't know. You just have that look about you."

"What if I were a doctor?"

"Then I might have pimped you out. You know, since the gas bombs dropped, there are many in need of your services."

"I'm sorry. I can't help you," Phil said, turning to the building.

The familiar sound of a gun being readied assaulted him like a physical blow. He froze. "I think we have a misunderstanding here."

"You're going to help us. I have a woman down the street that is in serious need of a doctor. Now either you come with us or I will pull this trigger and we can see what happens next."

Before Phil could respond, he felt something splatter on his back like a crazed artist throwing paint at a canvas.

"Run!" another young voice said.

He turned to find the threatening youth lying on the ground without a head. His compatriots scurried away like frightened mice on a sinking ship.

"I suggest you enter now, while you still can."

Phil turned to the voice. An ancient-looking man stood on top of the stairs leading to the brownstone. His body shook, but he steadied himself with a golden cane. He had no weapon, but something told the doctor that he was an imposing force to be reckoned with. The old man pointed to the sky with the cane.

"We better hurry. The eye in the sky can hold them off for

only so long. Soon, these thugs will be back with reinforcements."

"Who are you?"

"My name is Midas Mink, and I need your help."

The old man waved him in. Phil ascended the steps and
entered the brownstone.

CHAPTER 9

Where am I? Where's Enyo?

Treeka stood alone in a white, wide open space with no windows, doors, floors, or ceilings. She was in a space so blank that there was no room left for anything else. Just Treeka.

"Eliza, are you there?"

As she enunciated the words, she heard them leave her mouth, but they didn't carry. It was like she was in a place devoid of sound. She knew her heart was racing, but not even that sound could be heard. Treeka raised a hand, then the other. They were perfect. Her hands glided across her chest. Instead of finding one breast, she found two. A feeling of hopeful exhilaration was overwhelming. She was whole. A wave of shock overcame her as she examined her naked form. It was a perfect construct, not a true image of who she really was. It was a mirage. In the distance, she could see someone. She was too far away to make out any details.

Who is that?

She strode toward the shape that resembled a person. The space she was in wasn't hot nor cold, but of perfect neutrality.

Meanwhile

Doc Chop stood before a series of monitors with a view of almost every corner of the city. He switched views so fast the images blurred.

"Where has she gone?"

"Are you asking me, master?" Melvin, his AI, said.

"Yes, Meeka hasn't checked in. It's been far too long."

"Her last known location was at the residence of Mr. Mink."

"She was supposed to pick him up at the hotel. How'd she end up at the residence?" Dr. Sylvester said to no one in particular.

"A struggle ensued between Mr. Mink and Meeka."

"Not even allies can be trusted anymore."

Dr. Sylvester fidgeted with his tie. Moments later, he removed it and threw it at the monitors. It clung to one of them.

"Melvin, can you please get Mr. Mink on the phone for me?"

"All the lines are down, master."

"Never mind, I have another idea."

Dr. Sylvester strode out of the room into the hallway. Drones buzzed overhead.

Soon, everything will be in place. The city will be ours!

He stepped through a labyrinthine passage descending into a dimly lit and unfinished tunnel system. People he referred to as his cybernetic enforcers herded through various passages. Nonsensical ramblings echoed throughout the hall.

"Dun-ditty-chik," one of the bound men said.

As the enslaved man was being hauled away, the doctor wondered who he could trust to bring back Meeka unharmed. Soon she was going to give birth to the first baby with a cybernetic data core. In time, he could transfer another human consciousness into the baby, giving the child the experiences of an adult.

Once perfected, we will make millions. Not to mention have the opportunity for immortality. But it doesn't matter if she dies.

"Melvin, how many men can we spare for a rescue operation?"

"All the men are processing the new arrivals. I estimate it will be several hours before we can spare anyone. May I make a suggestion?"

"What is it?"

"We should put the prisoners we captured earlier to good use. They are strong enough to handle any resistance that you might encounter at the Mink residence."

"That's too risky. Nozomi has been transferred into a new body and Rick is loyal to her."

"What if we used the carrot instead of the stick for a change? We might get better results?"

Dr. Sylvester thought of his brief but intense time with Meeka. He had never bonded with anyone. Not even his wife or daughter.

I have to save her.

After a moment of hesitation, he headed toward the holding cells.

Dr. Clemmant followed the old man through a hallway that descended to a well-kept basement. It was difficult to tell how large the space was because the walls were painted black.

"The lab's this way," the old man said.

"I'm sorry, I didn't get your name."

"That's correct. I didn't give it to you because it is need-to-know, but I think I can trust you with it. I'm Midas Mink."

The old man was spry for his age. He opened a hatch in the center of the room.

Am I seeing things? I'm sure that door wasn't there a moment ago!

"Down there," the old man pointed toward the darkened hole.

"What's down there?"

"Your patient. Now hurry up with the procedure. My old bones cannot wait much longer."

Dr. Clemmant examined the hole in the floor for a long moment. When he was certain that he would not get sucked into a black abyss, he crouched and used the hand holds to lower himself into the darkness. After several moments, he reached the bottom. He pulled a pocket flashlight from his coat. The space below looked like the house staff used it for storage, but after some fumbling, he found a switch. He flipped the switch into the "on" position. Lights flickered and a buzzing noise emitted from the fixtures, which he estimated to be older than him.

"I don't see anyone," Dr. Clemmant yelled.

His voice echoed through the chamber. He was about to yell again when he spotted a table behind some stacked boxes. He gasped as he gazed upon two of the most beautiful females he had ever seen. They were lying naked on stainless steel tables. A blond woman in her thirties and a younger Asian woman rested on the tables. The younger woman was restrained and appeared to be pregnant.

"What am I supposed to do with these women?"

"Operate on them, of course," the old man's voice said.

Clemmant looked around the room, trying to locate the old man.

"Stop wasting time looking for me. I hired you to perform a

simple task. You will induce labor on the pregnant cyborg and place the baby in the incubator. Its labor is premature, but should survive. Fail at this task, then you shall never see the light of day. Succeed and you shall be rewarded beyond your greatest imaginings."

"That's Martha! But how?"

"She's a beauty, isn't she? I got her just for you." The old man cackled.

"It can't be her—"

"It is her, just spread her legs and took at her tiddles."

"I don't understand."

"You soon will. Now, first things first: start inducing."

How can a cyborg give birth? I'm way out of my depth here.

"I cannot do this," Dr. Clemmant said.

A whirring sound emitted from the corner of the room. Moments later, a black drone hovered above. He noticed a canister attached to the bottom.

"You don't want me to have to spray you. I can compel you, but the results are never the same. My special recipe is not lethal, but I find that the subjects are never the same. Spare yourself the misery and just do your job. I will throw in a bonus for you."

"What kind of bonus?"

"How does another million sound? But only after you complete the task."

Dr. Clemmant checked the Asian girl's vital signs: all normal. He removed her leg bindings.

"What are you doing?" the old man said.

"I cannot deliver her baby when her legs are bound," Clemmant replied.

"Okay, but remember to tie her back up once the baby is here."

Dr. Clemmant finished his preparations and started the induction process. The Asian girl's screams echoed through the small makeshift delivery room.

"What are you doing?" the Asian girl said.

"I have induced labor. I'm going to require your assistance to bring your baby into the world. What is your name, dear?"

"Meeka! It hurts!!!"

"It will be over soon, but I need you to push—now!"

Meeka screamed as she tried pushing. The baby wasn't ready to face the world. But he took his time with his patient, and they kept trying. It was going to be a long night.

Nozomi paced the familiar cell. Her girth had grown in size so much that the cell seemed cramped. The torso was several sizes too large. This made the arms and legs she chose seem freakishly small.

I need more appendages.

"How are you holding up, my love?" Rick asked.

"We need to find a way out of here. Doc Chop isn't going to keep us alive much longer."

"He would have killed us already if that were true. I think he has some other sick idea in mind for us."

"Just be prepared to strike at my signal. He will pay for what he's done," Nozomi said.

"At least you were able to transfer yourself into a new body. I'm still walking around with a time bomb." The bars rattled as Rick struck them in frustration.

"Be quiet. I'm trying to think here."

She brought up her heads-up display and ran a diagnostic. Although her new torso had two arms and legs, it was elongated enough to support more.

A clanking sound echoed through the chamber. It was impossible to know from where it originated, as it seemed to come from everywhere at once.

Moments later, she met the gaze of the man she'd vowed to tear apart. He seemed to be looking past her.

"What the fuck do you want? Do you have some new torture for us to endure?" Nozomi said.

"Don't provoke him, Noz. I don't want my head coming off just yet."

Dr. Sylvester smiled. It was a creepy sight to behold.

"How do you like your new body?"

Nozomi shot him a hateful glance. Her right arm was numb, and it was difficult to stand for any length of time. The body transference procedure wasn't as successful as she had thought.

"It's fine!"

"I can help you harness the power of your new body. You'll be a force to be reckoned with. Imagine the look on Treeka's face when you tear her limb from limb with your eight arms."

"What are you talking about?"

"I can give you a much needed makeover, but I need something from you in return."

I don't trust him, but he is different. He must want something—bad.

"Tell you what. You give me that makeover and remove his bomb, and you have a deal."

The doctor opened both of the cell doors.

"I will fix you now, but we will wait to remove that bomb from your boyfriend's head until the task is done."

"I can live with that. But can you fix my arms and legs? I'm not doing so well with my current body."

"Follow me. You will like the upgrades that I have set aside for you."

"You never mentioned what depraved task you need us to perform," Rick said.

"Meeka has gone missing. Telemetry data suggest she is at the residence of a friend. But I have a bad feeling about it. Meeka can't fight in her condition."

"What do you mean? She's nearly kicked my ass many times, even when she was injured."

"She's pregnant."

"How is that possible?"

"Dr. Ash changed many things when she transformed you and Meeka. But your reproductive organs are intact. Meeka carries our child."

Nozomi laughed. She couldn't help it. The two people she hated the most in this world needed her help to save their baby. Doc Chop flushed, his jaw clenched, but he didn't show any sign of aggression.

"Are you going to help me or not? It's an easy job, especially for someone like you."

"Not so fast. If we help you, then you let us go, for good. No more strings."

The doctor seemed to consider for a moment before agreeing. He rummaged in a pocket of his coat and produced a bloodstained key card.

"This will give you access to the armory. Feel free to take anything you think you need."

Nozomi snatched it and motioned for Rick to follow.

▭

Treeka examined her current state. She was in a white space that seemed to go on endlessly. Her only anchor point was a mysterious shape in the distance. Since it was the only thing besides herself, she was drawn to it like a bug heading for a bug zapper.

What has Enyo done to me? She said something about merging with me or something like that. Maybe this person knows?

She had no way of telling how long she'd been in her current reality, but that didn't seem important. Getting out was, but who was she again?

I know I'm someone important, Enyo said as much. I must not forget my name. I'm Treeka! Argh, why is it so hard to remember?

She ran toward the shape as fast as she could. She tripped and fell toward the ground—but where was it? She had braced for the inevitable pain that someone had from falling, but other than a feeling of motion, she experienced nothing. A black tar substance covered the floor. The blackness was slowly dissolving. She couldn't explain it, but the more the black tar substance dissolved, the more difficult it was to remember her name or who she was.

"I'm losing my mind!" Treeka screamed.

Other than the same muffled sound, nothing else came back. Next to the black tar was a needle attached to a gripper. The device resembled an old-fashioned fountain pen. Treeka poked at the tar with the needle. To her astonishment, it stuck to it. She found it distressing that her name kept slipping away like a paper in the wind. She started carving the names that she could remember on the floor. But soon it was erased.

There must be a way to keep my carvings.

She dabbed the tar with the needle, then started writing on her skin. Each stroke caused the most agony she had ever experienced.

This must be the way. If writing the truth is the only thing that will cause me pain, so be it.

Treeka screamed as she wrote her name and every other piece of information she knew was the truth. She loathed self-mutilation, but in this place it was the only true feeling she had known.

CHAPTER 10

Nozomi and Rick followed the doctor into a cylindrical chamber. Metal from the nearby walls was falling out of place. Exposed wires and conduit showed through the exposed metal.

"What's this place?" Nozomi asked.

"It's where the magic happens. Now get undressed and lie on the table," Dr. Sylvester said.

Rick gave her a guarded expression.

"I trust that you will keep an eye out. In case the doctor tries anything," Nozomi said to Rick.

The couple embraced. Even with her mixed-and-matched body parts, it was evident that Rick still wanted her.

That kiss tells me all. Perhaps I will keep him around after all.

"Now, we don't have a lot of time. Get on the table and we will start the procedure. I promise that you will be a new woman when you wake."

"I prefer to be awake during the procedure," Nozomi said.

"Even with diverting your pain receptors, you will not be totally without pain," Dr. Sylvester said.

Nozomi gave him a contemptuous stare.

"Very well then."

The procedure seemed to last an eternity. Nozomi diverted most of the pain away. It subsided, but never left. Pain that would have measured a ten was brought down to a two or three, but never exceeded a four. She watched in fascination as the doctor selected additional body parts with the utmost care. The most pain came from the limb transfusion method. He used a hot glue gun to attach additional limbs. She imagined that she was the subservient to the grandmaster of pain. She longed to drink from its endless wells of pain. Each sip was more electrifying than the last.

"Bring it on!"

The doctor ignored her cries and kept working. She experienced more pain in a single session that she ever had. A black angel of death appeared before her. Its ebony wings stretched out and enveloped her. She succumbed to the darkness.

Sometime later, Nozomi awoke to a blanket of pain. It was like someone wrapped her in bandages that shot electricity into all parts of her body simultaneously.

"You're awake, good! Now take two of these every four hours to stave off infection. These blue pills will help with the pain."

"What do I look like?"

The doctor tapped something on his tablet. The metal panels covering the wall inverted into mirrors. She looked like a beautiful insect with her eight arms and four legs. She stood atop the bed and took in her naked glory. Her breasts and pussy had a symmetry that took her breath away.

"I am beautiful."

Rick gave her an indecipherable look of anxiety. Nozomi extended her fingers, metal blades shot out of her fingertips. She took beep breaths as they retracted into her skin. The pain of unleashing her blades was overwhelming, but her cybernetic circuitry kept up with diverting the agony. At the end of the room was a set of leather clothes with cutouts to account for her multiple arms. Rick helped her fit into the rest of the outfit. He gently caressed her skins as he pulled the light leather over her exposed skin. A lustful urge almost overcame Nozomi.

I will fuck Rick to death once we are through with the doctor. Tonight, this ends.

Nozomi stretched her arms and legs. She found she was even more dexterous, with eight arms as two. Doc Chop was a master at reforging the human body.

If only he wasn't a psychopath, he and Dr. Ash probably would have gotten along.

With her instructions from the doctor, she and Rick left the underground chamber of Doc Chop's lair. She buttoned the raincoat that the doctor provided to hide her new body. She wanted to attract as little attention as possible as she became one with the night.

▭

The perfect white space was marred by Treeka's lifeblood. She looked back from where she shambled toward a mirage.

There was never another person, was there?

A zig-zagged line of her blood was the only tangible thing, besides the needle, in this entire place. The pain helped her remember what had happened and what was happening to her. Enyo was absorbing her mind. She didn't know where she was, but suspected it was a mind wipe chamber.

I must resist.

Flashes of metal caught her eye. The truth she poured into her arm by way of the needle, the more the real world was revealing itself. She carved "Meeka is my sister" into her thigh. The pain was excruciating, but the more truth she inflicted upon herself, her surroundings were revealed. She was lying next to Enyo, so close they were touching. A rubberized blob was attached to their faces. Tubes and wires were strewn around them. A robot, or skinless cyborg as Treeka called them, was typing something into a computer. The more Treeka carved, the more frantic the robot worked. "Tsuyoshi Kiyomizu was a good man," Treeka carved into the flesh of her calf. Her surroundings flickered in and out of existence like a strobe light. She carved one final message in her stomach "Doc Chop is a monster."

"I demand you to stop," the robot said.

The robot wrapped its metal fingers around Treeka's neck and squeezed. This felt more like a physical attack. Treeka snapped out of it and the world came into full view.

That's it! Time to stop the mind wipe.

Treeka pulled the robotic fingers from her throat, they snapped like twigs. The robot pushed her hands back. She screamed and metal rods shot from her wrists and penetrated the Robot's skull. Its head exploded in a series of sparks and after a brief flame fell lifeless atop her.

Midas Mink was hunched over the laptop in his study which he referred to as the time capsule. The room resembled something out of a 1940s detective noir film. All it needed was a chain-smoking gumshoe.

"Fucking moron," Midas yelled to no one in particular.

The surveillance footage was in black and white, and it only had a limited range of motion. The basement and livery areas of the house had its blind spots. He enjoyed watching people squirm and this Dr. Clemmant was rattled. His ring which resembled a bloodshot eyeball had the uncanny way to stare down people. He realized it years ago after he'd won it from a gypsy in New Jersey. Every time he entered into negotiations back then he'd most always had a favorable outcome.

I'd better not rattle the doctor too much, he might blow a gasket. He is a little high strung after all.

Midas flipped between the various camera angles and stopped at the inner door of his converted cellar.

Maybe that stern talking to was a bit much for that young man. He's acting irrational.

A clanking sound interrupted his train of thought.

"Intruder alert," a robotic voice said.

Has someone broken in?

Midas pressed the button on the laptop assigned to change the view. He was pressing so rapidly the screen wasn't keeping up with his clicks. The screen froze on the feed in the foyer. A man and woman were visible in his hallway. Midas opened his right drawer and removed the hand gun. He seized the controls to his motorized wheelchair, it jolted forward then stopped. The motion almost threw Midas out of the chair.

Easy old boy, it's best not to get rattled. You've dealt with scum like this before. Footsteps echoed on the wood floors and staircase. The intruders were coming upstairs. Probably to get to him.

I'm not going to make it easy for them.

He positioned himself near the top of the stairs. That way he would see the intruders before they saw him. Moments later a lone female with an oversized raincoat and sunglasses ascended the stairs. She froze at the top of the stairs. Clearly she wasn't expecting him to be there.

"Hello, lover. Are you ready for your tuck-in time?" the woman said.

What the fuck is she going on about?

"You're trespassing, now get out," Midas said.

"I'm yours, I want you to insert all you have into me."

Midas pulled the hammer back on the gun. "I don't know who you are, but you've got ten seconds to get out of here before I pull the trigger."

"You wouldn't hurt the woman who is going to give you a blow job. Now would you?"

"What?" Midas said, confused.

The woman opened her raincoat. Two flawless breasts and a neatly groomed pussy was visible. She licked two of her fingers then played with the loose skin near her pussy. Soon her fingers were deep inside. She moaned. "Does that old cock still work?"

"Who are you?"

The woman dropped the raincoat and positioned her four arms and legs into a squatting position. One hand pleasured herself while the other three kept her from falling.

"Don't you want to see what it's like to fuck a freak?"

Midas had seen his share of freaks in his day, but she was a new kind of savory delight that he had yet to taste.

Who is she?

"Your friend Dr. Javitts sent me, and I have been a naughty girl."

"He already sent SoMay; it's not like him to send another so soon."

The woman nodded then a scream echoed through his private chambers that startled him so much he dropped the gun. It went off. An intense pain like no other coursed through his leg. The android he knew as SoMay ran through the hallway screaming. Her hair was on fire.

"It's amazing how lifelike robots are these days, a man's voice said."

A moment later he came into view. Midas's eyes were drawn to his hands. They were burning.

Dr. Clemmant couldn't believe the bloody mass of flesh, blood, bone, and electronics he had brought into the world. He wrapped the infant in a towel, then raised it to the camera.

"It's a boy!"

The baby screamed. The electrodes lit up with an array of tiny LEDs. At a glance, it looked like the baby had a rainbow across its head. Splotches of hair grew around the electronic strips. The baby's cries became shrieks.

My ears are ringing. I need to find a way to shut this kid up.

Dr. Clemmant crouched and put the baby on the floor and covered his ears. He hated putting a baby on the floor, but in his haste, he had forgotten to secure a crib. The monitoring equipment and incubator shattered.

"Take control of the situation, doctor," Midas yelled into the microphone.

The old man's bellowing would have been deafening if the baby hadn't already achieved that feat.

"Give him to me," Meeka said.

As soon as Dr. Clemmant put the baby into Meeka's arms, the cries stopped, and it cooed. Meeka exposed her only breast, and the baby fed.

"No, no, no! You fucked up, doctor. You weren't supposed to let that baby near that tramp. You are through; you will never see a penny. I'm sending a man down to take care of you. Now get out of my sight."

Meeka laughed.

"It looks like you chose the wrong employer, Doc. I'm sure that Sly has a job for you if you survive."

Dr. Clemmant ran to the nearest door. It was locked. He looked at one of the cameras; the glowing red light mocked him. He pulled the door with both hands; it didn't budge.

"If you want me out of here, then open the door."

"The other doc is coming for me, lover boy," Meeka taunted.

Clemmant paced around the room, combing his hands through his hair. The old man sounded pissed, and he didn't want to meet any more of his men. On the other side of the room, he spotted a hatch that was built into the wall. He ran toward it and pulled. It stuck a little, but he managed to get it open. A narrow shaft greeted him. He estimated the drop was about fifteen feet to the bottom. A slamming noise came from the makeshift operating room.

"He's over there!" Meeka said.

He scrambled into the shaft. It was dimly lit, but he was able to make out an outline of a door at the bottom of the shaft. He heard footsteps from at least a half-dozen people.

I need to get the hell out of—

Before he could finish the thought, he felt a tugging sensation. He tried to pull himself downward, but his legs wouldn't obey.

I'm stuck.

Soon he was being pulled by an unseen force. Something latched onto both of his ankles and yanked him back up. He hit his head at the top of the door, his vision blurred for a moment. Two blurry shapes loomed overhead. As his vision cleared, two figures came into view. A tall man with an unkempt beard and a woman dressed in an oversized raincoat were staring at him.

"Is this the doctor who delivered Meeka's baby?" the woman asked.

"It's him all right," Meeka said.

"On behalf of our employer, we wish to thank you for your services," the woman said.

"Who are you?" Clemmant asked.

The woman laughed. "I'm your savior—or executioner. You decide."

Before the doctor could respond, the woman spread her arms, and the raincoat fell to her feet. She was naked and she rubbed her breasts and the rest of her body as if she were cold. To Clemmant's surprise, she seemed to grow two more arms and legs, giving her a spider-like appearance. She closed the space between them, and he groaned as her breasts and pussy rubbed against him.

"Ooh, don't you want me, lover?"

Clemmant scrambled back and let out a wheezing sound as he hit the back wall. The woman laughed as she unbuckled his pants with one set of arms and smacked him with the other two.

"You've been a naughty boy. Now tell me, who do you work for?"

"An old man that lives above here."

He screamed as she grabbed his balls and squeezed. His eyes watered as a dull aching pain settled in his groin.

"Stop! I will tell you everything I know," Clemmant said.

"I know you will," the woman said, loosening her grip.

She ripped his underwear off. He squirmed as his pants caught on his ankles. She stroked his penis, and he responded to her touch.

First she tries to rupture me, now she wants to pleasure me. What angle is this crazy bitch playing?

"I can show you a great time, lover. You don't mind, do you, Rick?"

"Nozomi, when have I ever denied you your fun?" the man said.

"You are a great lover. I want you to fuck me hard when this is over. I might let this one join in if he tells us what we need to know.

These people are whacked.

"Why does the old man want the baby?"

"He wants me to transfer his data core into the baby."

Nozomi's gaze settled upon the baby.

"The baby's head is too small for an adult data core."

"I—I developed a process to transfer the data core information without surgery."

"Interesting. Well, my employer will find that useful."

"Who is your employer?" Dr. Clemmant asked.

"Dr. Sylvester Javitts."

No, I cannot let Sylvester poison me again.

"What's wrong? It looks like you've seen a ghost."

"I think this is Sly's archnemesis or something," Meeka said from across the room.

"Well, then buckle up, because you're coming with us."

"I'd rather die," Clemmant said as he dove into the shaft.

He hit the bottom hard; something in his arm snapped. He screamed, and his body ached all over. Laughter echoed from above. Moments later, he heard the whine of a motor. He couldn't find a way out of the shaft. An outline of a door was visible, but there was no door handle. He was trapped. He pushed on the door with his good arm. It did not budge. A clanking sound reverberated as the whining became louder. Dr. Clemmant didn't see the object that killed him. The myth of seeing one's life before a dying man's last breath didn't come true for him. Just the crushing agony.

CHAPTER 11

Dr. Sylvester Javitts rarely stepped out of his clinic, but news regarding his bride and baby was of utmost importance. His heart fluttered while waiting for the door to open. He had been searching the city with his drones for days with nothing to show for it except a few sleepless nights.

The door opened and Rod, one of his lieutenants, waved at him.

"The path is clear."

"Are you sure that nobody is on the streets?" Dr. Sylvester asked.

"Positive. Now let's move before I get towed. It's late, but there might be some cops on patrol."

Dr. Sylvester followed Rod out the door and into the chilly night air. He couldn't remember when he last had been on the actual streets of New York. Probably not since he lost his wife. Moments later he was in the back seat watching the late night traffic on Broadway. He could not believe that one of his oldest friends would betray him.

He cannot have her, no one can.

About thirty minutes later Rod parked several doors down

from the home of Midas Mink, one of his oldest friends and business associates.

"This is the closest I can get you without double parking," Rod said.

"Wait with the car."

His lieutenant grunted in agreement. It was best to keep the car ready in case he needed to make a hasty exit.

The door to the residence was open. Dr. Sylvester didn't know where Nozomi and Rick were. The message they'd left was brief, but indicated that Meeka was alive. Screams echoed through the residence like ghosts haunting a distant past.

"I'd rather die," a familiar male voice said.

Is that Clem?

Dr. Sylvester picked up the pace. If his old friend was alive, he could use him to accelerate the timeline. After a brief descent down some stairs, there was a steel door. He heard screams from multiple people at once. He longed to be in the room. He relished seeing his old friend again. He opened the door to find his friend diving into some sort of shaft. Nozomi and Rick made no move to stop him. Meeka cackled. "Hey, Sly, you missed all the fun."

"Who was that man?"

"He's the doctor who brought our bundle of joy into the world," Meeka said.

A pang of guilt overcame Dr. Sylvester. He had known Dr. Clemmant for longer than most of the people in this room had been alive. He deserved a more dignified death. He vowed to make his sacrifice a meaningful one. Everything was going to plan. The police were too busy to interfere. Soon most of the people he had not controlled would be gone or under his control. Yes, all things considered, today was a good day.

Treeka threw the dead carcass of a skinless cyborg off her. Her skin was raw and hot to the touch and she had chills.

Am I sick?

Since awakening on Dr. Ash's table more than a year ago, Treeka had experienced many things, but she hadn't been sick since her awakening. Wires, tubes, and various sensors covered most of her exposed skin. As she removed the invasive objects from her skin, memories that were not her own surfaced. A flash of a girl with white hair entering a room invaded her mind like it was her own. The girl kneeled before an ageless woman wearing a kimono. The woman's face was pretty, but something about it was unnatural.

Treeka snapped out of it. She pulled the remaining wires from her body. She scanned the room for the woman who brought her to this place. Enyo was gone. Near the table from which she woke, Treeka found an envelope. As she picked it up, she noticed that it weighed a lot more than it should have. The word "Welcome Treeka" was inscribed on its surface. She opened it and an elegant hand-written note with a data shard caught her eye.

Dearest Treeka,

If you are reading this note, then your transformation process is complete and I have begun my journey. It has been many years since I found a worthy successor. Like you, I was also born of flesh, metal, and bone. We are not the sum of our data core, but rather are defined by our actions. You will find a data shard enclosed. It's keyed to your unique data structure and only you can access its secrets. I invite you to join me when you are ready to begin the next level of your training. Only you will know when you are truly ready. But until then, please use this knowledge for good.

Fair well until we meet again.

—E

Treeka finished dressing, then examined the data shard. Dr. Ash had not told her about these before.

How do I access the information?

Until she deciphered the riddles of the notes, she decided to tuck the shard into her secret spot in her belt for safekeeping. One truth remained: Doc Chop must die.

Dr. Sylvester watched his growing baby boy suckle the only breast of his cybernetic bride.

If I didn't know any better, I would think this child was several months old. Not a newborn.

"What's wrong with Jerry?" Meeka said.

"Who's Jerry?"

"Your son."

"What makes you think there is anything wrong? I checked his vitals before we got into the car."

"He's growing—fast!"

"That's all part of the process, my dear. By next week, he will be old enough to be your brother."

"What? How?"

"It's part of the serum that I perfected. You're proof that it works. Jerry will be an important part in the battles to come."

Meeka wiped a tear.

"I told you not to get attached. He's more than a child. He's better because he will have a hand in making New York a haven for people like us. Nobody will look down upon us anymore. Instead, they will bow."

The car pulled onto West 65th Street and continued into Central Park.

"It's time to meet the troops."

"Are they ready?"

"The police have all but left the city, and the few pockets of resistance we've encountered fell quickly enough," Dr. Sylvester said.

"What about my sister?"

"She's already been dispatched."

Meeka shrugged. "Good, I didn't like that bitch much anyway. Now let me mind Jerry," she said, looking away.

She's crying. She does have feelings for her sister, and that is a liability, Dr. Sylvester thought.

Moments later, the vehicle pulled into an expansive parking lot. Beyond the lot, a massive field stretched on as far as he could see. He couldn't see much of the green because of the throng of people on and around it. A man in an Italian suit strode to the doctor. He was short, far below average height, maybe five-feet-five or so. His hair was slicked back. The look reminded Sylvester of a hungry used-car salesman.

"Hey, Doc. Here is everyone. Like you wanted."

"Thank you, Rodrick."

The man nodded, then rushed over to help Meeka with the car door. She was having a difficult time getting out of the car with the growing child.

"Whoa, when did you say this baby was born?"

"Just a few hours ago. He's my growing little monkey."

"He looks much older. If I didn't know better, I'd say he was at least a year."

"Is it ready?" Dr. Sylvester interrupted.

"Yeah, everything is in place. The podium is over there," Rod said, pointing to a raised stage.

The doctor strode over to the stage. Several pregnant women waved at him. He ignored them. He turned his gaze to Meeka. She was holding the ever-growing baby and appeared to be having a difficult time handling it. He didn't see the baby as Jerry, but rather patient zero. If he was a disappointment, then he had plenty of backups that were going to pop anytime now. He smiled to himself, then removed a piece of paper from his inside coat pocket. Hundreds of expectant faces stared back. Murmurs of nonsensical mutterings resonated through the crowd.

"Thank you for coming out on such a cold night."

Someone from the crowd hooted, another let out a moan. All of his enforcers were here with portable cattle prods. Some of the more vocal attendees were hit with enough voltage to make them scream. The others in the crowd cowered.

I wish I had more time to create all of you in my image.

"Tonight we shall make history. We have a common enemy that must be defeated. The corrupt politicians have turned this once great city into a cesspool of high taxes and corruption. We are here to liberate the populace."

The crowd cheered. He reached under the podium for a canister without a label. It reflected the dim light as he held it in his hand. Many of his enforcers did the same.

"Each one of you will take a can and several injectors. When you see a crowd of people, use the spray. If you see someone alone, use the injector."

Dr. Sylvester watched as his enforcers unboxed and handed out cans and syringes to the crowd. They passed them out quickly.

"When you liberate the citizens, our numbers will grow. They will automatically return to this place for supplies. It might take days, weeks, or months, but soon we shall liberate the people from the evil that runs it. Now let's save the people before the bad men come."

The crowd roared and scattered. The neurotoxin may have turned their minds into mush, but once a person breathed in the gas, within a few hours they instinctively found their way home. Doc Chop gazed upon a giant box with vents that emitted a pheromone that would make the infected come back every twelve hours. New recruits would be outfitted with the same weapons as the others. The gas would flow until everyone in the city was under his control. He checked his watch. It was almost time for his injection.

I can't turn into one of these raving lunatics. That would not do, not at all.

"You did it to yourself, old boy," Dr. Sylvester said.

"Yeah, you certainly did," Rod said.

He strode back to the car. Meeka seemed stressed. The baby appeared to be two years old.

"Boss, what should I do with the others?" Rod asked.

"Take them to the lab and have the doctors induce labor. It is time that this youngster has some siblings."

Rod nodded and headed toward the pregnant women.

"I thought I was special?" Meeka said in a pleading tone.

"You are, my dear. Jerry needs some playmates, and there's plenty of me to go around. Now we need to go to the lab and get ready."

"Ready for what?"

"Soon men will be coming, and I have a surprise for them."

Dr. Sylvester Javitts cackled. Meeka gave him a wary look. Rod opened the door for the couple, and moments later the doctor watched in fascination and delight as his minions did his bidding. Gangs of his infected attacked people and sprayed the canisters while howling at the moon. Everything was going according to plan.

Doc Chop removed his new tablet from its case and scanned through the information that Rod uploaded to it. Everything was so complicated now that all communications were down.

Dr. Sylvester pulled up an offline map of the area. Using the annotation features on the tablet, Rod circled the properties that would provide the best view of his staging area. If there was going to be any resistance, it would be here. He was confident the local police weren't going to be a problem, but the New York State National Guard was another possibility. His hundreds of neuro-compromised specimens would not last long against trained soldiers. He picked up his handheld radio.

"Doc to exterminator," Dr. Sylvester said.

"I'm here, boss," Rod said.

"I need you to see if Will Scrutchers is available."

"Do you have any idea where I can find him? It's not like I can pick up the phone."

"He's on Roosevelt Island. Look for the construction site on the south side."

"Roger that."

If that meddling cybernetic bitch is still alive, these beasts will find her.

CHAPTER 12

Treeka stared at the lifeless body of Enyo one last time before leaving the transformation chamber. She thought about the data shard that was left for her. She had no idea how to access it.

Eliza!

She accessed her cybernetic interface. It was unresponsive. But upon closer examination she noticed a microphone icon with a circle and a slash going through it. She tapped on it.

System Message: *All sensory input has been disabled for your protection. Now that the danger has passed, would you like to enable these controls?*

An answer with a green "yes" button and a red "no" appeared before her. She tapped on "yes." Moments later, her usual cybernetic menu appeared.

"Treeka, you're alive," her AI said.

"You sound surprised. Were you expecting otherwise?"

"Oh, no. I had every faith in your abilities. Did you need help with something specific?"

"I need you to analyze something for me," Treeka said, holding up the shard to the light.

"You are holding a data expansion card. While it's properties are similar to that of a data core, the shard is keyed to a specific person's DNA."

"How do I install this shard?

"Show it to me," Eliza said.

Treeka held up the shard to the light and gave the AI permission to access her senses. Her heads-up display filled with information. An area on her upper neck near the base of her skull highlighted and magnified.

"There is an access point at the highlighted area," her AI said.

Why haven't I noticed this before?

Treeka scratched at the skin on her neck. She pushed around the area—nothing.

"I can't access the area to insert the shard."

"You cannot access the interface without performing surgery, and the interface port must be kept clean during its insertion; otherwise it won't work. We need to create a sterile environment."

"Just tell me what I need to do."

"We need to find a suitable area to perform the operation."

Eliza gave Treeka a list of needed supplies and some suggestions where she could find them. Supplies in the immediate area were scarce. The inner door to the lab didn't seem to work. A touchpad was the only visible access point. She touched the cold smooth surface of the pad. A white back light appeared with an outline of a hand. She placed her right hand over the outline. A negative-sounding chirp and an Access Denied message appeared on the touchpad.

"How am I supposed to get past this?" Treeka said in a frustrated tone.

"It's logical to assume that Enyo or her robotic assistant have access to the panel."

Treeka gazed upon the dead cyborg and her robotic

assistant. A pang of guilt overcame her as she gazed upon Enyo's body. Like her, she was just trying to survive. A long, slender, perfect-looking arm dangled motionless near the table. Her eyes settled upon her hand. She hurried to the table and examined the body, which was riddled with several tubes, wires, and straps. Treeka pulled as many out as she could find, but the body still wouldn't budge.

"How am I going to break her free of this infernal machine?"

"You could try to remove her hand," Eliza said.

Treeka was reluctant to mutilate such a perfect cybernetic body. Enyo's frame and figure were even more perfect than Nozomi's. But she had to get to Doc Chop before the city was overrun with toxic nerve gas. She took Enyo's hand. It was as smooth as glass and was firmly attached to her arm. Treeka did her best to remove the cyborg's clothes to gain better access to her shoulder area. Her olive skin was smooth to the touch and didn't have a blemish. Like Nozomi, her breasts and genitals were more perfect than those of a supermodel.

Perfection is the enemy of my kind. Many of us look so inviting, it makes us targets for the depravity of men.

After spending several moments examining the area for a way to detach the arm, she noticed something in the robot's hand. It was a pointy-looking instrument that resembled an awl. Treeka pried it from the robot's dead hand.

This will do.

It broke her heart to mar the beautiful cybernetic specimen that was Enyo, but she put those feelings aside as she stabbed and pulled the hand free. Several minutes later, Treeka placed the less perfect hand of Enyo on the access pad. The purple milky substance didn't affect the electronic lock's operation. The door slid open. Another room with the equipment she'd expected from a hospital operating room was present. She opened many drawers and cabinets before she found the required supplies.

"Are you sure you don't want to reprogram that robot to assist in the surgery? It might not be wise to do this on your own."

Treeka thought of all the near-death experiences she'd had with machines and decided to trust her fate to her own hands.

"I'm not alone, Eliza. I have you."

Treeka gave full control over her body to her AI. She didn't trust herself and needed to be as precise as possible. The surgery didn't take as long as Treeka expected.

"I will need to recycle your neuro circuitry in order to bring the shard online. Do you approve of this action?"

"Wait. Is there any way to tell if this thing is malicious? Like with a malware checking system?"

"Not without a diagnostic console that is designed to read such devices, and the code contained within them. But if there is anything potentially harmful to your circuitry, I'm programmed to isolate it. Do you want me to proceed?"

"Yes, let's get on with it already."

Treeka thought recycling her cybernetic interface would be like falling asleep. She'd experience a brief nothingness, then awaken with whatever new upgrades she was supposed to receive with the shard.

Treeka opened her eyes to an expansive grid of nothingness. Black tiles with thick white lines could be seen for infinity. She took a hesitant step forward. As she stepped on the black squares, they came alive with activity. She thought she could make out patterns of circuit traces.

System Message: *Expansion chip diagnostic in progress. Functionality at ten percent.*

An image of a microchip materialized out of thin air. It formed eyes, a nose, and lips.

"Hello, Treeka, it's Eliza. Your autonomous intelligence, or simply AI for short."

Treeka took a step back.

"Can't you take the form of something a little less creepy?"

"Don't like my true form?"

Eliza's eyes and lips separated from the circuit board. They seem to float in front of the cartoon shape like one of those creepy office program helpers.

"It's not what I pictured."

Eliza changed into an animated manga style shape with modest features. She seemed to look at her blue wireframe features, then snap a finger and changed to a three-dimensional female with a black leather uniform.

"Better?"

Treeka nodded.

"What is this place?"

"Technically, we are just bits in your mind-space, but I call this the 'in-between,' the area between sleep and being awake. We are only fourteen percent finished with the diagnostic. When we get to twenty-five percent, a diagnostic console should become available to you."

"What am I supposed to do with that?"

"It's a just a construct that will allow you to access the data within the shard. There is a lot to process, since your usual boot time is less than a millisecond."

"How long will this diagnostic take?"

"Hard to say, but I can do a little math. We are approaching fifteen percent, and the elapsed time has been six minutes and six seconds. Assuming the same level of processing power to achieve the same result, we are looking at six-point-six-six minutes to complete the cycle."

In the distance, gigantic shapes formed. To Treeka, they resembled mountains.

"What's happening over there?" Treeka said, pointing at the newly formed cluster.

"Your mind is filling in those blank spaces. Your subconscious is painting the landscape to help you visualize the space we're in now."

Treeka watched in fascination as the mountains grew, and trees and waterfalls materialized. It was like someone was painting a vista at record speed while she watched. Soon, the beautiful scenic vista was invaded by skyscrapers and a dense city landscape. Black clouds formed and rain began falling. An icy breeze chilled Treeka.

"Why is this place becoming so—dark?"

"Your mind is generating this. I'm not a psychologist, but it might indicate your state of mind," Eliza said.

A gray obelisk shot through the floor like an excavator boring to the surface. A computer terminal and monitor grew into existence.

"You may now access the shard directly."

Treeka took a hesitant step toward the terminal. As she approached, the monitor came to life. A login prompt appeared. It reminded her of homework. She studied for hours and remembered being on her laptop for many hours at a time. She cringed at the memory.

"How do I access the information?"

"You can begin by typing your name," Eliza said, as if it was the most obvious thing in the world.

She typed *Tomiju* and received an Access Denied message. She tried her full name: *Tomiju Kiyomizu* to the same effect.

"Stupid machine!"

She tried her nickname of Treeka. The system came alive. Information appeared on the monitor so rapidly it was difficult to make out what it was.

"Can you slow it down?" Treeka asked.

"Let's try something else," Eliza said.

Moments later, the empty grid in her immediate area came to life. Images of people and places she didn't recognize appeared. It was like looking through a window into someone's memories. They streamed past like paper caught in a wind. An image of a young girl climbing a mountain appeared in lifelike detail. It was like she was on the mountain with her. A flash of light, then an image of a young woman, perhaps a little younger than herself, stood before thousands of figures dressed in all manner of battle gear. Some wore simple robes while others wore suits of armor that appeared medieval. Others were in black leather. Another flash was so bright it blinded her. As her vision adjusted, an older woman sat alone in the center of a darkened room. She wore a nightgown that was opened, revealing bare skin with round holes.

Enyo!

The woman rose, then removed her nightgown and examined a slew of round holes around her torso. A tattoo of a serpent was just above her more private area, its head resting between her breasts. The woman stretched out her arms and metallic arms attached to body armor latched onto her effortlessly. A kimono was wrapped around her and a metal hand gave her a traditional straw hat. She held out a hand and a blue Katana was thrust into it. She waved, then turned to walk away. Several similarly armed men and women dressed in black ninja outfits followed her. The images were replaced by a Diagnostic Complete message.

"The system is online. You now have full access," Eliza said.

A floating three-dimensional file structure filled her vision. As she touched a folder, it illuminated, and an image appeared above it. Treeka surmised it was a visual filing system. As she reached for an image, what was contained within filled her vision. She opened a folder containing weapons, assassins, and shields. A map of the world appeared with several piles of weapons, with locations in New York, London, and many other places on the globe. She touched the assassins image, and red dots filled the map.

There must be thousands of assassins.

She paid particular attention to the ones listed in New York.

"These people and resources await your command," a male voice said.

"Who are you?"

"I'm Ike, your personal assistant."

"What happened to Eliza?"

"I got rid of that unwanted malware. It was getting a little crowded in here, don't you think? It's just you and Ike here now."

"What the hell is going on here?" Treeka said.

"I'm minding the store while Enyo is gone. How can I help you, Treeka?"

"Are you a part of the shard?"

"Yes, as are you. I think your time would be better spent gathering resources for the coming battle. If you don't agree, I will follow your lead. I'm here in an advisory capacity. You have the final say on how we should proceed," Ike said.

"Proceed with what?"

"The battle for New York, of course. Doc Chop has infected fifty-seven percent of Manhattan already."

This AI thinks I'm a general. How much time has passed?

The grid turned red and alarms blared. It was like her ear was against one of them.

"Someone has breached the perimeter. I suggest you leave mind space immediately," Ike said.

Treeka understood what Ike was talking about. It was

obvious that mind space was her virtual world. She brought up her cybernetic interface. The shard gave her more options. She selected the Exit option. The lab came back into view. Red lights were flashing everywhere. The room shook from an incessant pounding. Something big was trying to get in. Light shone in from the direction of the pounding. It wouldn't be very long before whatever was pounding would be inside. Treeka braced herself for the inevitable as she searched fruitlessly for something with which to defend herself.

CHAPTER 13

Doc Chop gazed upon an older luxury building with an expansive outdoor balcony. Massive entry doors and a manicured garden were some of the features the doctor enjoyed.

"I'll take this one," Dr. Sylvester said.

The building was the nicest on the block. Rod checked his tablet. "This has been one of the world's most luxurious resorts since 1899," Rod said.

"I'm sold!"

"This one's occupied. It will take some time to clear. I don't think the residents will go willingly," Rod said.

"Leave that up to me. Now get your men into position."

Rod pressed the button on his radio. After a brief chirping noise, someone answered.

"Bruno here. What can I do you for?"

"How many enforcers can you spare?"

"I have three or four, but since it's the end of the shift change, I have a dozen."

"Get all available enforcers and brutes to the Delphie Hotel overlooking Central Park South immediately," Rod said into the radio.

This building is close to the Fifty-Ninth Street station. I bet

I can find a tunnel here. With this, we can survive a prolonged siege.

"Oh, a Will Scrutchers called. He said that the next batch of beasts is en route and should dock at Kip's Bay this afternoon."

"Good. Send in the Beastmaster and his crew."

"Already on it; over and out."

"It won't be long now. With the reinforcements from Dr. Scrutchers, we shall be an unstoppable force."

"Excellent. Do you have any blueprints on that tablet?"

Rod swiped a few times.

"This building is too old to have a digital copy, but there is some information on it in my database."

"How are you accessing it? I thought the internet was down."

"Before the collapse of communications, you tasked me with an alternate relocation plan. I thought it was prudent to hack into the New York Realtor Association database. I have detailed information, floor plans, and maps of the entire area."

"Excellent. Does this building connect to the tunnel system?"

After some frantic swipes and grunts from Rod, the mobster showed the doctor a map of the subterranean portion of the building. An underground speakeasy was featured.

"This building is old, so there are most likely some hidden nooks and crannies to be explored."

Moments later, a horde of enforcers, infected, and brutes controlling dozens of drones crossed the street and lined up behind the doctor. A horn sounded in the distance, which reminded Dr. Sylvester of a shofar.

"I think we are ready for breach," Rod said.

"Wait for the general," Dr. Sylvester said.

"I think he's coming now," Rod said.

Another horn blared as an enormous beast that resembled a rhinoceros carried a group of bald men. The man in the lead stood atop the rhino. The streets were mostly deserted, but the ones who had dared to leave their hovels ran to shelter. Another man shot fireballs toward people. The leader pulled back on the reins. The beast roared and bucked. The men on the rhino's back were knocked to the street below. A man hiding behind a wrecked car ran away. One of the bald men let out a tribal scream then raised his hands toward the running man. Moments later electricity shot from his hands and enveloped the running man, who let out a blood-curdling scream.

"All right, enough fucking around. Get over here," Rod said.

The bald man with the mohawk leaped off the beast and strode toward Rod.

"I don't answer to you."

"Rourke, over here. We don't have time for fighting among ourselves. Later I will treat you guys to a round in the pit. But for now, we have other priorities," Dr. Sylvester said.

"Yes, boss," Rourke and Rod said at the same time.

"I have a challenge for you guys. The one who brings me the most scalps or newly infected will become my new number one. This position has many perks and responsibilities. I will grant you a special title as well."

"What title?" Rourke asked.

"How does the Baron of New York suit you?"

"I like the sound of that, mate."

"The rules are simple. Each of you will take odd or even floors. Whoever comes out with the most bodies wins," Dr. Sylvester said.

"Also, to make sure we have a level playing field, Rod will only be allowed to use syringes to convert people. You have thirty minutes to prepare, then the fun shall begin."

The door was pummeled by a seemingly unstoppable force. Treeka couldn't find a suitable weapon. She stared at the scalpels on a nearby tray.

I might piss off whatever that is if I use that.

She grasped Enyo's arm tightly, like it would save her from what was behind that door.

"Might I make a suggestion?" Ike said.

"Please do."

"Within the shard you have access to the most powerful assassins known to man. I suggest you put them to good use."

"How? They won't follow me."

"You have access to the same information that Enyo had. All dispatch needs is the access codes."

"Step me through it, Ike," Treeka said as a hand reached inside for something to mangle.

The arm was muscular and hairy. It reminded her of a gorilla. Moments later the door gave way. She dodged the incoming door with ease. She missed her Katana, but she wasn't defenseless. She held Enyo's arm as she would a sword. She felt a little ridiculous defending herself with another person's arm, but she reminded herself that Enyo was no ordinary person. She was the head of the most notorious hit squad ever conceived. The creature came into full view. Its arms resembled those of a monkey, but its midsection was that of a serpent. The head was a bull. It was like someone had fused an enormous gorilla, a gigantic serpent, and a Minotaur. It raised its head and howled. The floor shook. It was like a stampede of buffalo was heading toward the lab.

"What the hell is that, Ike?"

"Camera feeds are down, but according to my sensors, dozens of people are heading to this place."

"We're trapped!" Treeka said.

Her voice sounded weak and unsure of itself. Doc Chop seemed to be a dozen steps ahead of any move she made.

"There's a private elevator that leads to the ground floor in the residence," Ike said.

"Guide me," Treeka said.

"Well, all you need to do is get past the abomination, then turn left."

Here goes nothing!

Treeka charged the beast. It raised its arms and curled its fists.

"Take me into overdrive, Ike."

Treeka ran toward the creature, then jumped. Her fist punched the thing in the chest so hard it slid between some scales and stuck. She slapped the creature with Enyo's hand. It damaged the creature more than she was expecting. The creature howled and slithered back. Her arm was stuck in its chest and the movement pulled her closer. She finally freed her hand, then she grasped Enyo's severed arm with both hands and cut into the serpent thing. It screamed and writhed. The giant gorilla smacked her.

"Ike, can you provide some assistance, please?"

"The center of the beast's circulatory system is to the right of your hand's current position."

"Thanks, Ike!"

The gorilla serpent roared as Treeka pulled piles of mucus-filled gunk to get to its heart. Her head slammed between the beast's hands, and she got closer. The beast punched and tried biting her as she squeezed what she thought was its heart. The organ exploded in her hands. A roar reading over a hundred decibels on her heads-up display deafened her. The beast toppled over like a leaf in the wind. She fell atop it as it collapsed. Tears welled up in its eyes. It moaned, and its mouth moved as if it had something to say. An intense sadness over-whelmed Treeka as the creature expired. She knew it wasn't natural, but a living creature must have had to give its life for this thing to live.

"What kind of strange shit has the doctor gotten us into?" Treeka said.

"I scanned its physiology during the fight, and despite its appearance, it's mostly human."

Treeka's face flushed as her anger rose.

"Doc Chop is going to pay!"

"The question I would ask is: How did it know to find you... if you were its intended target?"

Treeka's eyes shifted to Enyo's severed arm. The doctor could not have done so much damage alone. He must be working with someone. Treeka couldn't imagine.

As Treeka descended the tower a nonsensical muttering of the infected echoed throughout the stairwell. She snuck a peek from the top of the stairwell. People gathered near each door with a spray canister in hand. Enyo's lab was at the top of an old restaurant atop an office building, so there were twenty stories to cover. It was difficult to know how many infected there were in the stairwell, but if the previous few floors were a gage, then there were at least a hundred to either pacify or elim-inate. She preferred to knock them out instead of killing them for many reasons, but she hoped for a nonviolent solution.

"I checked the outside building camera, and the entrance is mobbed. I don't think we're getting out there," Ike said, bringing up various camera angles.

Many of the infected carried syringes and cans that resem-bled spray paint cans. She didn't see a way out of the building.

"Din diddie chickie," a voice said from below.

Treeka snatched a glance. Everyone in the hall stopped and pointed at her.

"Gee meree to-scape ginnee," several voices said in unison.

Moments later, all the infected charged up the stairs toward Treeka.

"I've checked all surveillance cameras in the building, and all the infected are heading here. The roof is your only hope," Ike said.

Treeka bolted up the stairs. Two stories up, the stairwell ended. The echoes of the gibberish language shot through her like a bullet. She opened the door and several infected had made it into the hall. Her presence caused a frenzy of confusion and pain for these people. Several tried stabbing her with various syringes. She battled them off with the only weapon at the ready, Enyo's severed arm.

"Go to the end of the hall. The next stairwell has roof access," her AI said.

She cold cocked people that attempted violence and pushed aside others. The second stairwell was much like the other, but she scaled the railings of the staircase to avoid the horde. She kicked in the outer door leading to the roof. An alarm rang out. There was no apparent exit, but a cluster of water towers were the only high ground. She glided over to them. A moment later she was atop the tallest tower. Cheers from an apparent gathering echoed through the buildings.

That's coming from Central Park!

She estimated that the building was at least twenty stories tall. Helicopters flew overhead. She tried flagging one of them down, but it didn't notice her. The horde of infected burst through the door.

Fuck—I'm going to die here!

About twenty feet away, an electrical box with the words "High Voltage" was painted on the outside panel.

I don't want to harm these people, but I need to stop the doctor.

She grabbed a pipe leading from the nearest water tower and pulled. Soon, cold liquid was spraying all over the rooftop. She ruptured several more pipes from the remaining water tanks. A wave of the infected rushed the water tanks. They pushed, but couldn't seem to cause any damage. Treeka jumped toward the electrical box that was on a landing just above the tanks. She pulled one of the cables loose and dropped it in the water. Moments later, everyone on the roof let loose the most horrific scream she'd ever experienced. Tears streamed down her cheeks, and the infected tried avoiding the charged water. Soon bodies floated across the flooded rooftop. She collapsed at the base of the panel and wept.

CHAPTER 14

DELPHIE HOTEL, New York City

Doc Chop gazed at the piles of bodies that Rourke had produced. Twelve piles of twelve brought him an impressive 144. Rod's infected count had reached more than a hundred.

"Congratulations, Rourke. You're my new number one. I've already told Bruno, and he will give the other generals the good news. Now, I need you to head over to Kip's Bay and receive our newest allotment of exotic reinforcements."

Rourke bowed before Dr. Sylvester, then mounted his cybernetically enhanced rhino, which let out a roar as it rampaged away from Doc Chop's newest base of operations.

"Burn the bodies, then meet me inside. I want a tour of my newest apartment," Dr. Sylvester said.

***

Treeka didn't know how long she'd been on the rooftop. Light shone from the building and illuminated the area. She estimated the sun had set over the horizon an hour earlier. She found the emergency electrical breaker and shut power off to the building. She trudged through the sea of water and charred remains. The water had seeped into the stairwell. Painful moans echoed through the hallways. The remaining infected put up a little resistance as she made her way to the bottom.

"According to my offline maps, you're approximately eight blocks from the crowd. Did you want to investigate?" Ike asked.

About ten minutes later, she approached Central Park.

"Ike, do you detect any cellular signals? We need backup."

"Negative, but I do detect a citizens band channel active in the area."

"Please tune me in."

Her AI narrowed in on the frequency. She thought she heard a familiar voice.

"Narrow in on that voice," Treeka said.

Was that Nigel?

"Milford Rogue looking for Charming Rat—over!"

"That's Nigel, I need to reach him."

"I've changed the frequency. Try to communicate now."

"Nigel, this is Treeka—"

"Remember, you're on an open channel. Plus you need a handle. Don't use real names or anything that can identify you," Ike admonished.

"Milford Rouge, are you there?"

An audible clicking noise, then silence.

Treeka ran toward Fifth Avenue and 65th Street. Taxis and cars were strewn across the street like an abandoned kid's toy chest. Clusters of infected roamed the street. They chased people as they left the safety of nearby buildings. A female infected leaped on the back of an old man and stabbed him with something. He fell face first onto the ground. Moments later, he picked himself up and wandered aimlessly toward Central Park.

"There's an old telephone booth nearby, at the zoo. It still may be operational," Ike said as he brought up a map on her heads-up display.

She decided to give it a try. If she could reach out to the Society, then she could use Enyo's code to call in reinforcements. Treeka increased her speed. Barricades prevented any more movement toward the telephone. She slowed her movement, but it wasn't enough. She slammed against metal and concrete and was knocked to the ground.

"What the—"

"Hold it right there," said a male voice with a Scottish accent.

She shifted her gaze to the direction of the voice. An older man with a full beard and a shotgun greeted her. She raised her hands.

"I'm not here to harm you," Treeka said.

"Whatcha doing, then? No bother."

The man held out an arm. She took his hand. He was stronger than she was expecting.

"I'm Shamus, ho might you be?"

"Treeka—look, I'm in desperate need of a phone. Does that one work?" She pointed to the booth next to the zoo entrance.

"It did, but I don't know who is going to call. There's not much left of the city."

"Do you hear that?" Treeka said, pointing to the park.

"I don't know or care. I keep to myself and people leave me alone."

"That's the sound of an army that's about to march."

"Where do you suppose they will be marching to?"

Over you if you don't help me, old man.

"There's not much left of the city's infrastructure. Police

have abandoned us, and whatever hasn't already burned will soon."

"Then you best get over there and make your call, missy."

Treeka strode to the glass and metal booth. Most of the glass was shattered. The receiver was off the hook. She picked it up and put it in its cradle. She picked it up again and could hear a single tone.

"We've got a dial tone. Now follow these instructions to the letter," Ike said.

"Which number am I to dial?"

Ike gave her the information. She dialed a series of numbers as an automated system kicked in. Finally, he instructed her to hang up.

"What did we do?" Treeka asked.

"Soon, that phone will ring and it will be dispatch. You need to recite the correct phrase when asked."

Moments later, the phone rang. It was louder than Treeka was expecting. She jumped, then picked up after the third ring.

"Repeat after me," Ike said.

Text overlaid her cybernetic interface.

"Command Echo Delta Fifty-niner," Treeka said.

"Operator three-five-seven speaking. It is an honor to speak with you, madam. Are you ready for the seed phrase?"

"Affirmative."

"I'm a dirty icicle in the shady north. What am I?"

"Black Carbon."

"What do you require, number one?" the operator asked.

"I—need—"

"Tell the operator that you are in need of backup," Ike said.

A flash of a memory that was not her own overcame her. A woman in her early twenties appeared, kneeling before someone. The woman gazed at an unknown master with a dogged look of determination. She raised her palms. Moments later, a slight curved blade of a Katana was placed in her hands.

"What are you waiting for? Tell the operator what you need!" Ike said.

Treeka snapped out of it.

Was that Enyo?

"I'm deep within New York City—I need backup."

"What's gotten into you?" Ike said to Treeka privately.

She ignored the AI.

I must be tapping into her memories—are our data cores linked somehow?

"I have a read on your location. Southeast Central Park. Is that correct?"

"Yes, but how many reinforcements can I count on?"

"There are no suitable candidates available. But the New York National Guard is en route to Central Park. The location isn't far from your current location. Is your situation dire?"

"Indeed it is."

"Go to these coordinates and wait."

Treeka hung up the phone.

"I don't know what you're up to, but if the National Guard is going to crash the party, then we're doomed."

"Why? Isn't the National Guard soldiers?" Treeka asked.

"Yes, but Doc Chop isn't stupid. His men will be on the lookout for any troop movements. He will be gone long before they can get there. Besides, we can't afford the National Guard seeing you. Given the current state of affairs, they are liable to shoot you on sight."

"What do you propose?"

"You need to lie low until I can find an alternative."

"The operator gave me a set of coordinates."

"You don't want to go there."

"Why?"

"That location is in Sakura Park, known to harbor the most notorious criminal element. You will not be safe."

"It's illogical for the operator to send me to a location that is unsafe for me."

"I will keep an eye out. Now let's move."

Broken glass at the bottom of the phone booth rattled.

An earthquake? No, surely not here.

"They're coming," Shamus said.

The older man looked like he had run a marathon. He bent over and panted like a dog.

"What is?"

"The unholy horde. We need to go—now!"

The old man ran and jumped behind an outcropping of bushes.

"I think we should follow that old man's lead," Ike said.

"What are you talking about?"

"According to the surveillance cameras that still function throughout the city, an unstoppable force is coming. It's best to get out of sight."

Treeka ran toward an enormous tree and grabbed the nearest branch. She leaped to the trunk and scurried to the top. Her mouth went slack as she took in the onslaught of activity. People with metallic arms and legs rode several animals. An enormous rhino led the charge. A bald man with half a face jockeyed the beast toward Shamus's barricade. Moments later, a smacking sound reverberated in her ears. Excited nonsensical murmurs followed.

"Itty, bun'cade formalla?" one of the infected questioned.

A lion stopped short of the barricade and roared. One of the infected tried to run, but the beast caught up and ripped some flesh off its neck. The man screamed as the lion continued its meal. Several other beasts ran past the barricade. Shamus screamed as a hyena tore into his back.

"No!"

The creature let out an evil laugh as it pounced. Treeka watched the remaining throng of creatures head toward Fifth Avenue.

"What the fuck was that?" Treeka said.

"It would appear that those zoo animals were being controlled by that bald fellow somehow," Ike said.

"Was it the gas?"

"Possible, but their movements were a little too precise. Someone has modified them."

"Doc Chop is behind every unnatural event that has happened since the attack," Treeka said.

A pang of guilt and regret overcame her as she descended from her high perch.

"I'm heading to Sakura Park to meet whomever the operator has sent over. We are few and Doc Chop is growing an army."

"You're Enyo's chosen; and if anyone can stop this madman, it's you. Which is all the more reason why you need to keep a close watch as you make your way to the park."

She decided to avoid the streets as much as possible as she delved deeper into Central Park. She didn't know what danger lie ahead, but she was glad that Ike had her back.

CHAPTER 15

Treeka made her way to the provided coordinates. A gazebo with holes in the roof was nearby. A misty fog rolled in, reducing visibility for much of the park. Cherry blossom trees were visible from the gazebo. She ducked under the gazebo as the mist turned into a light rain.

"I don't know what you're worried about. I haven't seen anyone in a while."

"It doesn't mean that they're not watching. I detect movement in a nearby building," Ike said.

Treeka shot a glance toward the entrance of a nearby building. A small man with a hunched back rummaged in a nearby garbage can. His matted, dirty hair fell over much of his face. A cat meowed loudly and rubbed against the man who appeared to be having a conversation with the feline. Treeka adjusted her auditory sensors and adjusted for noise generated by the light rain and wind.

"I know she's powerful, Clara I just hope she's worth it," the man said as he emptied the contents of the trashcan on the ground.

The cat ate something out of the pile and looked toward Treeka and continued to cry.

"The great mother has spoken for this one. Uncle Nigh will test her all right, yes he will."

"That man is obviously insane," Ike said.

"I wonder," Treeka said.

She strode toward the man who'd started organizing the trash into neat, categorized piles.

"Are you here for me?" Treeka asked.

The man shot her a nervous stare.

"How that is desired? What plan do you entail?" the man asked.

Is he one of the infected? He hasn't tried to stab or gas me yet, so probably not.

The man continued his sorting and muttering. Treeka couldn't understand the man, and after a few minutes of watching him sift through the trash, she decided that he wasn't her contact.

"What now?" Ike said.

Treeka shrugged, then strode to the gazebo.

"The operator sent you, did she not?" the man asked.

She shot the man a concerned look.

"I know you are not her because she's the one who saved me. But you have her essence."

"This man knows something."

Treeka kneeled to get a better look at the man's trash pile. As she examined the heap, it seemed to spell something. She leaped onto the nearest light pole to get a better view. The letter "E" was visible.

"There are too many coincidences, Ike. This man knows something."

"I don't think so. We should probably leave," Ike said.

"Don't go. The man inside your head is deceiving you. Let me help you find your true potential. I shall."

The man turned and met Treeka's gaze. His emerald eyes

were captivating. She got a better look at his face. He seemed familiar somehow.

I know I've seen him before, but where?

"We have been watching for quite some time, my dear," the man said.

The cat responded with a meow.

"Don't let her interfere," the man said in a harsh tone of voice.

Does this man have a split personality?

"No, she's with Enyo. She must follow Ninell, yes. The nice woman's in danger."

"He will judge. Take her before him," another voice proclaimed.

The man seemed to hold a conversation with several others. He waved at her. Against her better judgment, she followed the man into a foreboding-looking structure.

"I advise against following this man. He's leading you into a trap," Ike said.

Treeka ignored the AI. She didn't like how it made Eliza disappear. The man's crazy babble started to make sense. The inside of the building looked like someone had set a bomb off. The walls were peppered with small holes. It looked like someone attacked the walls with a baseball bat. Treeka flipped one of the nearby switches. No light, just an audible clicking sound.

"The path lies through here. Yes it does, Ninell."

The man pointed at various parts of the building's interior like he was giving a tour. He opened a door at the end of a hallway and stepped inside. The room was illuminated by several opened windows. The man ducked behind a piece of furniture that resembled a desk. A creaking sound echoed through the room as he opened a trap door. He descended into darkness without another word. She heard his incessant mumblings as he moved farther into darkness.

Let's see where this rabbit hole goes.

Treeka enabled her night vision as she descended into darkness. She could see the man shambling ahead. She followed him into a side room.

"It's her," a female voice said.

Treeka followed the voice. It was Anya Middleton. The woman who led Treeka to Enyo.

"Did Ninell do a good job?" the garbage man asked.

"Yes, you did fabulous," a male voice replied.

The garbage man appeared to be looking everywhere at once. "I—I did my part. Can I have payment?"

The man chuckled. She couldn't see the man, but she had a bad feeling about him.

Ike, I need to you enhance his face, Treeka said privately to her AI.

I cannot do that, dear; he will delete me if I do.

The man in the shadows tossed a knapsack toward the garbage man. He opened it and removed a human head. Its left eye was missing. To Treeka, it looked like it had been shot through that eye. Ninell removed a flashlight and probed the eye socket with a finger.

"Don't worry, the data core is intact. Now, leave us."

The garbage man left without another word.

"So, is this the cyborg who killed Enyo?" the man asked.

"I did not kill—"

"Shut up until you're spoken to," the man interrupted.

"I brought her to Enyo. She was the last person to see her alive," Anya said.

The man came closer to Treeka. The scent of sweat and yesterday's aftershave turned her stomach. His enormous frame reminded her of wrestlers with bulging muscles. He wore a full suit, was clean shaven, and had a buzz cut, which reminded Treeka of a military man.

"Who are you?"

"You may call me Agent Six. I'm the Society's number one. Your improper use of Enyo's codes activated me. Depending on your answers, you have precious minutes left in this world."

"Ask me anything you want. I will answer truthfully," Treeka said.

Agent Six stared at her for a long moment. It was like he was trying to will the truth out of her.

"Tell me what happened after Enyo rescued you from the subway."

"Rescued? I was abducted."

Treeka relayed every detail since her forced induction into the Society. She left nothing out. Agent Six seemed unmoved by anything she said.

I'm not going down without a fight.

"Enyo was obsessed with finding the right one."

"What are you talking about?"

"We've been aware of Doc Chop's activities for quite some time. Until recently, the Society had no reason to kill the doctor."

"What changed?" Treeka asked.

"Shortly after your encounter with that beast at Rockefeller Plaza, Enyo received a job to kill the enemy combatant known as Doc Chop. So, when Enyo learned of you, the decision was made to bring you into our group."

Treeka's jaw clenched. "I never had a choice in the matter."

"That's true. For thousands of years the Society has done everything in its power to keep world peace. Most superpowers use us to maintain plausible deniability. And we always deliver."

"It sounds like we are on the same side, so why don't you help me kill that fucking doctor?"

"I would love to, but you have assimilated our leader and taken her data shard for your own. Your actions constitute an act of war."

"How many times do I have to tell you? I'm not the one who initiated that. I'm not your enemy."

A chirping sound emanated from the man.

"What is it? I'm interrogating the prisoner." The man listened for a long moment. Treeka tried to use her enhanced hearing, but Ike kept those controls on lockdown.

"Doc Chop has made his move. It seems that both of us have no choice but to work together."

"I am ready to lead the assault."

"Not so fast. Since you contain the sum of all Enyo's thoughts and experiences, you will provide assistance. We can't afford to lose you in battle."

"How many do we have?"

"More than enough to get the job done."

"Are they cyborgs?"

Agent Six gave Treeka a wary look.

"Enyo was the only one within our ranks."

"Then I hope you brought plenty of gas masks for everyone."

"Each member of the Society has a portable respirator in case of emergencies."

"If I'm not going to be fighting, then how am I to help?"

"You will be fighting, but not in the way you think. You will be installed back in the control center, where you will have access to all our resources."

"No, that's not good enough. I need to be there when the doctor takes his final breath."

"You may have Enyo's knowledge, memories, and experiences in that shard. But you're not our leader," Agent Six said.

"He has my baby sister under his spell. I need to ensure her safety."

The man gave her a stone-faced look. She couldn't read him, but he didn't look amused.

"We don't want innocents to get injured. We will bring you in physically once the threat has been eliminated. That's the best I can do."

"I will do my part, but I have a request," Treeka said.

"What is it?"

"I need you to bring back Eliza, my AI. I don't trust Ike."

Agent Six was silent for a long moment.

"It will be done. Now come with us. We need to prepare for the battle to come."

She didn't relish the thought of these people taking the doctor down without her. She dreamed of stabbing that son of a bitch in the heart herself. But she had the opportunity to bring him down for good.

Meeka and Doc Chop strode into the penthouse apartment of the Delphie Hotel. An expansive view of Central Park and the city beyond was visible.

"Don't you love the Art Deco style, my dear?" Dr. Sylvester said.

"It's nice," Meeka said.

Jerry, their one-day-old child, had grown considerably. He ran around the apartment like he was four or five.

Men moved the red and gold furnishings out of the apartment.

"Someone grab that kid before he gets hurt," one brute said.

"Jerry, come on over here. I have a toy for you," Meeka said.

"It's time for Jerry to go to school, dear," Dr. Sylvester said as he waved at the child.

"Da-Da," Jerry said.

He leaped into his father's arms.

"Where are you going?" Meeka said.

"I need to run some tests at the lab. I shouldn't be more than a few hours. This apartment has an excellent view of the park. Why don't you rest a while?"

"I'd rather crack some skulls."

It's probably best to keep her busy while I test Jerry's capabilities.

"I'm going to drop you off at the lawn in Central Park. I need someone to check the perimeter to ensure that our staging area is secure. Feel free to crack as many skulls as you can find. There are bound to be spies lurking about."

Meeka gave him a look of excitement. She bent over and gave Jerry a kiss on the cheek.

"Listen to daddy, I will see you at dinner little guy."

Bruno doesn't need any help. But at least I gave Meeka a purpose. Now it's time to see what Jerry is made of.

About an hour later, Dr. Sylvester sauntered into his lab. He was in a good mood and was ready to test the limits of his baby. A flash of memory invaded his consciousness. A young girl played hide-and-seek in his workspace. She loved playing in his lab, but the doctor hated entertaining the child. There were too many experiments that she had disrupted during those moments. He had vowed never to have another child, but it was different this time. Jerry would go well beyond the limits of human capability. It was too bad he wouldn't live.

Meeka is going to be devastated, but we will have another child. Maybe we will have it the old-fashioned way.

The child played on his sensitive equipment.

"Jerry, sit in the chair—now!"

The boy stopped at the outburst, then cried.

"Shut up! It's time to take it like a man," Dr. Sylvester said.

He poked young Jerry with another batch of his stem cell cocktail. Moments later, the child began screaming.

CHAPTER 16

Treeka followed Agent Six and Ayna Middleton out of the building and into the afternoon light. The rain increased to a slow but steady drizzle.

"The lab overlooks Central Park West, so we should be able to get a good view of Doc Chop's assembly," Agent Six said.

"So, what is your plan?" Treeka asked.

"The lab has a supercomputer, which you will have full control over. From there, you will have access to the city's closed-circuit camera system. You will be our early warning system."

"Each member of the Society has a radio link that has full access to the major events and disaster channel. Our radios are encrypted, so you don't need to worry about anyone listening in," Anya said.

"Once Doc Chop's forces are sufficiently reduced, you will join us for the trial of the century," Agent Six said.

Treeka didn't like the idea of being away from the action, but she reasoned she had the most important job of all. She knew Doc Chop's tactics better than the Society did, and with access to a supercomputer she would be unstoppable.

Treeka stepped out of the elevator and gasped as she took

in the condition of the lab. It had been restored to its original condition. She cringed as the computer interface came into view. Several doctors and lab technicians busied themselves at workstations. A woman of average height approached. Half of her head was shaved; the other half had several shades of pink, purple, and blue.

"I'm Rocket, the technician in charge of your well-being. I will monitor your vitals while you're connected to the terminal."

"What weapons will I have access to while connected?" Treeka asked.

"We have a few dozen robots at our disposal. We were able to piece them together after your battle at Rockefeller Plaza. You will be able to directly control them."

"How many troops do we have?"

"We have three hundred and eighty-six in the greater New York area. Several hundred more are traveling to the region."

How many does Doc Chop have?

"What is the estimated enemy force?"

Rocket looked away. Her expression changed immediately. Treeka knew the situation was grim, but the technician's reaction didn't give her hope.

"Are you ready for immersion?"

"Will I be fully aware of my surroundings?"

"Yes, you will have access to all connected cameras inside the lab. As well as several connected closed-circuit systems."

"Then I guess I'm as ready as I will ever be."

The technician handed Treeka a bundle of clothes.

"Put these on. The suit works best when it is against the skin. You can use the bathroom..."

Treeka removed her clothes in front of the technician and put on the skintight suit. It was made of an elastic material. Sensors appeared to be built into various areas throughout the material. Treeka sensed the woman was attracted to her. She ignored the leering and finished putting on the matching gloves and boots. The virtual reality headpiece rested in her hands. She gazed upon its shiny exterior.

This interface was different from Enyo's. Perhaps she knows.

"Rocket, Enyo didn't need a VR headpiece. Will I have the same full-immersion experience?"

"It will be no different. As I understand it, you have the same cranial interface, so you should see everything the same."

Treeka put on the VR interface. The familiar black tiled grid was spread out before her. Her heads-up display had several options. She chose monitor. The empty space filled with various views around New York. Each was labeled.

There must be hundreds of locations.

Treeka zoomed out, a map of the city and the five boroughs was displayed. Hundreds of dots appeared almost everywhere on the map. She pulled up a few locations to test the interface. She tapped on the location for Central Park. A smattering of dots appeared throughout. She zoomed in on the zoo area. She could see the wrecked barricade where Shamus had made his last stand. Treeka's heart sank as she thought about the old man. He'd only wanted to protect his few remaining belongings. Now he was dead. She opened several more locations: the traffic circle at Columbus Square, Seaport Village, and another dot that was hovering over the city. A spectacular aerial view of Manhattan was visible. She expanded the view, and it stretched over all areas. It was like she was dangling off the source of the image. She took a few more minutes to get adjusted to her new surroundings.

"Treeka, it's Agent Six. We're in position near the doctor's lab. Can you tap into any of the cameras here?"

She tapped on the agent's dot on the map and zoomed in. Several camera icons appeared nearby. She tapped on all the cameras. Real-time views of the entire area surrounded her. She could see the burly agent and Anya. Both crouched on a staircase that led below a market.

"I see both of you."

"All right, see if you can tap into any other cameras in the area."

Treeka found and selected the Scan Camera option. Moments later, a series of dots appeared. She tried to access one of the cameras in the building that Agent Six was entering. She flipped through various camera angles until she saw Doc Chop, who was doing something to a child. The camera angle was positioned at an angle that made it difficult to clearly see what he was doing. She tried zooming in, but the camera was unresponsive.

"I've found him," Treeka said.

She flipped through all the cameras in the area, but there was no sign of Agent Six or Anya.

Where did they go? Is it a blind spot?

Each monitor flashed a nasty red with a single message: "WARNING: Data Breach Imminent."

"Eliza, what's going on?"

"It appears that you've tapped into an infected closed-circuit system. As a precaution, the command center has been firewalled," her AI said.

"Can I get a message out?"

"All communications are currently down."

"What about the citizens band?"

"That's currently open."

"Can you relay a message?"

"Whom shall I call?"

Treeka gave Eliza a series of instructions. Her AI and everything else in her sphere of influence went offline. The familiar black and gray tiles reappeared. A message floated in three-dimensional space in front of her. As she read the message, a sense of hopelessness washed over her. Moments later, her entire world went offline.

Dr. Sylvester Javitts examined his child.

"You're a part of something big, my son. Something larger than you or me. We will change the world, together, as father and son—your sacrifice will not be in vain."

The doctor poked the child with a large syringe. Blood drained into a series of tubes. He labeled each sample, then bandaged the wound.

"What sacrifice?" Meeka said.

"Well—hello, dear. How long have you been there?"

"Long enough." She started loosening Jerry's straps.

"Get off of him, bitch," Dr. Sylvester said.

She shot him a hateful look.

"I love you, Sly, but I won't let you kill Jerry—argh!"

Dr. Sylvester back-handed Meeka so hard, she stumbled and fell.

"You bastard!" Meeka said.

The cyborg threw a series of knives at Doc Chop, and he raised his arms in defense. All but one of the blades missed him. Two enforcers grabbed Meeka. She clawed, bit, and punched. Jerry cried and reached for his mother. One of the men grabbed Jerry. The child bit him on the arm and peeled back the skin. The man let out a shriek. Two other men came into the room and one of them punched Meeka in the stomach. She let out a wheezing sound, then began to cry.

"Take her away."

It took three men to restrain her.

"Where should we put her?"

"Let her cool off in the indoctrination chamber."

Meeka screamed as they carried her off.

Dr. Sylvester sighed as he held his son. *She will come around—I hope. If not, I have several other mothers-to-be impregnated with my seed.*

Moments later, a tall bald man entered the chamber.

"We have intruders," a man's voice said.

Dr. Sylvester shot a glance at the voice. A skinny man held a camera in his hands.

"Is that your intruder?" the doctor said, pointing to the camera.

"No, of course not. But I have captured the intruder's location."

"Tell me more."

"With the internet down, there's only one viable option left. Our closed-circuit camera system."

"If it's a closed-circuit system, how can someone hack it?"

"Most systems communicate over the internet. But there are several private citizens who take part in a private network that spans the entire city. Apparently, we're connected to that. I was able to lock them out. But guess what?"

The doctor shrugged.

"I ran a trace that got me a valid IP address. It took me only a minute to figure out its location."

"Let me guess; it's somewhere in Manhattan?"

"It's near a building in the Columbus Circle area. Do you want me to assemble a team?"

"Yes, take some enforcers and brutes and bring me the person responsible."

"It shall be done," the skinny man said as he left the lab.

The doctor examined Jerry. He had grown several inches and his hair was shoulder length.

He's aged another nine months since he's been here. Fascinating!

He took his son's vital signs, then looked at his watch. He had been in the lab for hours and had nothing to show for it.

"Time to get back to the lawn and rally the troops. It's almost time," the doctor said to the empty room.

"Time for what?" a gruff voice asked.

Moments later, something large and metallic hit him. He tumbled to the floor.

—

Sumoto reset his router and protected the firewall. His internet connection had been going down all day.

The border gateways are up. This must be a local problem at the perimeter. Time for a field trip.

One of his clients who wished to remain anonymous had contracted the hacker to breach certain networks, and the money was too good to pass up. He grabbed his laptop, an extra Ethernet cable, and shoved the items into his messenger pack.

This was going to be a long night.

He opened his door when his landline rang. He froze. This was the second time the phone rang within a week.

Is Treeka trying to contact me?

He rushed to the phone and picked up. A series of clicking sounds emanated from the phone. To Sumoto, it sounded like a relay inside an old public switching office.

"Urgent message from T—ree—ka. Need help—hack—rest —tower in Col—um—bus Cir—"

The line went dead. He knew when a computer was trying to contact him. Treeka had gone missing days ago, and he could not find her. The words *rest* and *tower* could only mean one thing: a restaurant in a tower. He remembered going to a cool revolving eatery down the street from Central Park, close to Columbus Circle. He used to go there with his friend Hiroto years ago.

I think a detour is in order.

Sumoto ran into the rainy evening with the only weapon he knew how to wield.

Dr. Sylvester snatched a glance toward the intruder. A burly man with no neck dressed in a nice suit pointed a rather large weapon at his head.

How did he get in here? It's time to punish my physical security staff.

"Don't look at me," the burly man said.

The distinctive sound of a trigger being cocked echoed through the space. The doctor raised his arms.

"Can we work something out?"

Dr. Sylvester risked another peek at the intruder. Then the fists came.

Sometime later, the doctor awoke strapped to his examination table. A light blinded him.

"Who's there?"

"I've finally found you. You will pay for what you did."

"I'm sorry, I don't understand," Dr. Sylvester said.

I sound like a weak, whimpering fool. I'm going to carve this man's testicles off and dine on his entrails.

"You experimented on her. I loved her."

"Maybe if you tell me who I harmed, perhaps I can make amends."

More pain shot through the doctor's temple. He blinked blood out of his eyes.

"Her name was Enyo. We were to be married. But that ended when you transformed her. Now she's dead."

Who is Enyo? Does he mean Eunice?

Dr. Sylvester's eyes glazed over as he pulled a long forgotten memory from his cranium. When he was working thirty-six-hour shifts at the emergency room, a young Japanese woman came in with stab wounds. After tending to them, he learned that she was a member of a fighting club. He didn't think much about it then, but later, when she lay bleeding in that cold dark alleyway, he decided she would be one of his first transformations.

"She wasn't called that back then. Eunice came to me after I found her bleeding to death in an alleyway. A victim of the very thing that you represent. I offered salvation, and she came willingly."

The burly man continued punching Dr. Sylvester until he could barely see anything. "Stop it, Agent Six," a female voice said.

"Anya, what are you doing?" the agent said.

A wet thwapping sound followed by a gooey spray splattered against his face.

"It's me, Daddy."

Dr. Sylvester turned his head toward the voice. He could barely see her, but could it be his baby girl after so many years?

Treeka gazed upon the vast emptiness before her. Unlike her previous experience, when Enyo had attempted the forced merge, the dead space seemed to fold in upon itself. She couldn't reach past an arm's length.

"Eliza? Are you there?"

All sensory input was cut off as invisible walls pressed

against her skin, but stopped short of crushing her. She curled into a ball and waited for the inevitable.

What will happen to my body once I am virtually crushed?

Treeka closed her eyes, and a flash of memory took hold. She let herself become immersed as she was transported back to a simpler time. Tomiju and Misato sat at a table with teacups and half-eaten anpan. They were dressed up to celebrate an occasion. She remembered that her father's backyard was the perfect location to celebrate anything. Light shone from the nearby garden and enveloped the sisters in a warm radiance. They promised to look out for each other—no matter the cost. Misato presented a miniature blue bonnet to her sister. She explained that her stuffed bunny wanted her to have it and it would remind her of their special bond. Tomiju gave her sister an image of a cherry blossom that she had made during art class. Of all the images Tomiju had created, this was Misato's favorite. The sisters embraced.

Is this the end?

The pressure on Treeka's body increased. Virtual simulation or not the confinement was becoming unbearable. All air escaped the small space. She felt like a bug trapped behind a layer of glass. Treeka couldn't believe that Meeka and she had drifted so far apart.

I wonder if we still share a telepathic connection. I've got to try.

She projected the feeling of her favorite childhood memory to Meeka. She hoped that her sister would get the message. Her vision blurred as she surrendered to the light.

CHAPTER 17

"FULL SENSORY INPUT RESTORED," a female voice said.

Treeka lay flat on the black tiles. Out of the corner of her eye, a flicker of light emitted. Soon, the entire floor was pulsating below her. The pressure lifted, and she raised her head to take in the ever-changing expanse. The video feeds restored. Even with her superior cybernetic interface, she couldn't keep up with the flood of input. Video feeds from around the world poured in. She tried to focus on the New York region, but the controls were inoperable.

"Eliza, can you help me?"

"Yes, that is what I'm here for."

"The system is stuck. I can't control it."

"An override has been put into place. I cannot manipulate it from inside the simulation. You must disconnect from the virtual reality interface before you can reset the system."

Treeka attempted a log out action, but it was blocked.

"I can't disconnect from the system."

"It seems that the command center has been infected with some sort of computer virus. I will short out your virtual reality helmet, and you will be disconnected immediately. But you may not be able to jack back in."

"I don't care. I need to stop whatever is happening before it crashes with me inside it."

Moments later, all sensory input was cut off. Muffled sound began to seep in. She removed her VR helmet. The inner lab looked the same. She put her hand against the touchpad. To her surprise, it opened. The outer portion of the lab was practically destroyed. Live electrical wires hung from the ceiling. Lab technicians and other helpers lay motionless on the floor. Blood pooled beneath the fallen victims.

"What happened?" Treeka asked.

"It appears that the command center has suffered an attack. I suggest that you arm yourself and prepare for anything."

Gunshots rang throughout the complex. Treeka couldn't find any weapons, so she smashed the glass of an emergency station and wrestled a fire extinguisher out of its case. A group of men with guns clustered at the end of a hallway. She ducked behind a cart and turned on her enhanced hearing.

"I can't find that cyborg bitch anywhere," one man said.

"Have you checked the inner lab?"

"It was locked," another man replied.

The men started moving in different directions. Treeka stayed low as a tall, skinny man approached. He moved past her and entered the inner lab. She crept behind him, then grabbed the man from behind and positioned her arms around his neck. He choked and coughed, then moments later he was out. She checked various drawers and closets for something to tie him up. She found some tubing and tied him to an office chair. She gagged him with a bloody shirt she'd liberated from a fallen lab technician.

"Wake up!"

Treeka punched the man several times until his eyes swelled. As he regained consciousness, he struggled and tried to scream. She punched him in the stomach. He wheezed then doubled over.

"I'm going to take this out of your mouth. If you scream, I will kill you. Is that clear?"

The man nodded.

She removed the gag. He coughed, then spat blood.

"It's you!"

"The question is: Who are you?" Treeka asked.

"I'm Bruno."

"How did you find this place?"

"It was easy enough. Our hacker traced your IP here."

"How? The internet is down."

"Something about using the private camera network is all I know."

"Who do you work for?"

"Javitts. He hired us to find you."

"What is he planning?"

The man laughed. "Do you think you can beat him? You can't win. He's built an army that's ten thousand strong."

"Where are they?"

"The lawn near Sheep Meadow in Central Park."

Treeka punched the man again; he was knocked unconscious.

"The cameras on top of the building can confirm his story. I'm pulling the feed now," Eliza said.

"Wait, I'm not hooked to the machine."

"You don't need to be. I figured out a way to tap into the shard without it."

Treeka's cybernetic interface was filled with images from the camera's feed. Several time-lapse photo loops showed massive crowds at the lawn area that the skinny man had mentioned.

"Even with the help of the Silent Assassins Society, we are

outnumbered. But when accessing the data shard, I found another way to defeat our enemy."

"How?"

"On top of this building lies a bomb with several explosive charges. While it's not enough to cause physical damage to the building, it will cause an electromagnetic field that will render all electronics useless. This includes the circuitry in all cybernetics."

"This will kill me, too!"

"Fortunately, Enyo, your predecessor, built the inner lab area to withstand a direct blast. You can still observe the launch and detonation from inside this room—until the cameras get destroyed."

"Meeka's still out there, I've got to find her."

"Let's keep that as a last resort."

"Very well, but I strongly suggest you use this weapon while you can. Once they mobilize, then it's too late."

Treeka glanced at the camera feed. The telephoto lens was able to zoom in within fifty yards of a stage, which was surrounded by thousands of people. A giant screen projected overhead so faraway participants could see the action. Doc Chop strode onto the stage. He waved. He looked like he'd been in a brawl. Both of his eyes were bruised.

What happened to him?

Moments later, Meeka was herded onto the stage, her hands tied. Treeka's heart sank as she saw the duress her sister had experienced. The doctor spoke to the crowd, but she didn't know what he was saying; however, the gigantic image of Doc Chop made it possible for her to read his lips.

"We've made great progress today. I've secured strong allies and found traitors among us."

Anya Middleton, the agent who had ambushed her, appeared on stage.

"I present my daughter. I thought she was dead, but she saved my life today and has joined our cause."

Treeka's heart sank as the doctor took her hand and raised it high into the air.

"She will have the honor of dispatching a traitor in our midst."

The camera centered on Meeka. She was bound and blindfolded. Treeka watched in horror as Anya Middleton decapitated her sister. Her head bounced off the stage, and the doctor applauded.

"No!"

Treeka collapsed to the floor. Her vision blurred as tears poured from her eyes. She couldn't breathe.

"I'm so sorry," Eliza said.

The skinny man stirred, then met her gaze. His expression changed. He turned pale.

"I... can help you."

Treeka grabbed the nearest heavy item and beat him to a bloody mess, then kicked his body outside the inner lab. It was time to end the madness; it was time to eliminate Doc Chop.

Sumoto traced the call to a tall glass building overlooking Columbus Square and Central Park. As he closed the metal box containing the switched telephone equipment, he glimpsed at something interesting. He craned his neck to get a better look. There was a radio tower on top of the building. The setting sun made visibility difficult, but he could see a metal oval tube was being pulled up the tower.

What is that?

Traffic was sparse, so he repositioned himself in the street to get a better look. Since the collapse, few could afford a vehicle, and the ones who did retrofitted them with armor and weapons. He did his best to stay hidden. He removed his smartphone and zoomed in on the tower. It was a cylinder with metal wires wrapped around it. The device reminded him of a Tesla coil.

It can't be!

An orange explosion gave way to a purple and white electrical blaze of light that filled the entire sky. His cell phone sizzled in his hands and lights flickered out. Transformers exploded. Soon, the darkness enveloped him and the rest of the city.

It took Treeka a week to find her sister's head after the EMP explosion. She didn't know if her sister's data core was still intact after the blast, but she hoped it was. All the drones and cybernetic implants embedded in people's flesh were fried in an instant. Tears of joy rolled down her face when Jonny D found her. He had survived the onslaught of the insane and infected horde. He had barricaded himself in an old bomb shelter and organized the neighborhood patrols using an ancient ham radio. He'd barely survived.

The giant hand painted posters of her across the city had both reaffirmed and encouraged her. Treeka didn't know who painted them, but it served as a reminder of her responsibility to the people. It would be a long time before the city would be back to normal, but she pledged to help in any way she could. Most of the world seemed to have left Manhattan island to its own devices. In the months after the EMP explosion, neighborhood patrols were established. Very few were able to cross boundaries.

Many of Jonny D's people had taken up leadership positions in the various neighborhoods across the city. Sheriff's or constables were established to keep the peace. Bounties for violent criminals or out-of-control cyborgs spread like wildfire. Precious metals, old vacuum tubes, or any other materials to service the many CB or ham radios still operating were some of the new currency. But basic supplies to sustain life were the most valuable.

It was almost impossible to get out of the city once the meat beast's dead man's switch was activated. But Treeka was able to find passage on an ancient tugboat that a heavily armed gentleman was operating across the Hudson. The man had recognized her. Her exploits against Doc Chop's minions were legendary among the locals and she was one of the few cyborgs that were able to travel freely in the machine-free zones.

"Even though your part machine, you're more human than many unmodified nowadays," the man had said.

Those words encouraged her to move on toward the quest for Doc Chop and his daughter, who all but disappeared after the blast. After many months of searching and interviewing survivors, she finally had a lead. Treeka tracked them to a dilapidated old bar with the words Scouts Irregulars spray painted on the entryway. The building had seen better days. All the windows were shattered. Bits of glass were peppered throughout the path leading up to the establishment.

I finally have them now.

Treeka crouched behind the remains of a burned out vehicle. She would wait for just the right moment before setting things straight. She unzipped the duffle bag that contained her preserved sister's head. The smell of formaldehyde was a pungent reminder of how precious life was to her. She lost everything to that crazed doctor and his daughter. She unsheathed the Katana and removed the sharpening stone. She wanted to ensure it was sharp for the moments to follow.

CONTINUE THE ADVENTURE

I hope you enjoyed reading **Silent Assassins Society**.

To receive an exclusive sneak peek into Treeka's next adventure I invite you to join my reader group. To sign up use the "Contact Us" form at https://www.davidgoodinauthor.com or https://cyberhunterorigins.com

ACKNOWLEDGMENTS

Developmental Editing by Mat Machin
Copy Editing by Micheal McConnell
Proofreading by Beth Doward
Cover Design by Konstantine Designs

Special Thanks to my advanced reader and launch teams.

ABOUT THE AUTHOR

D. B. Goodin has had a passion for writing since grade school. After publishing several nonfiction books, Mr. Goodin ventured into the craft of fiction to teach Cybersecurity concepts in a less-intimidating fashion. Mr. Goodin works as a Principal Cybersecurity Analyst for a major software company based in Silicon Valley and holds a Master's in Digital Forensic Science from Champlain College.

Requiem - A Dark Journey (Fall 2022)

Interstellar Online
Blast Off
Cassidy's Fleet
Cosmic Squeeze (Fall 2023)
Sol-86 Academy: The Return of Megabot